Keira at Stageschool

Gardine Sinclair

Chapter One

It was one of those days that just seemed too hot to do anything. It was so warm in the classroom that Keira longed to put her head down on the desk and sleep. Maths had never been her favourite subject and today not one word Mr Lucas said made any sense. The chalk made irritating noises on the board, a cloud of dust rose from the board rubber every time someone made a mistake and a bluebottle drummed lazily against a window. The smell of thirty-two bodies all sweltering in their school uniforms was not a pleasant one and Mr Lucas was eventually forced to open a window.

This proved to be too much of a distraction, especially for those sitting nearest as the sounds from the playing field, where some lucky class was enjoying cricket or rounders, were a hundred times more interesting than angles.

Keira, her chin resting in her hand as she propped herself up on her elbow, was able to gaze out of the window without drawing too much attention to herself. Sat at the back of the class, as she was always considered one of the "sensible" ones, she found her eyes drawn to the daffodils that bobbed about in the garden between the classrooms and the playground.

She watched them in fascination. Like dainty maids in golden, frilly caps they danced about joyfully, their faces turned to the sun and Keira wished she was out there dancing with them, instead of being stuck in this stuffy room with another twenty-five minutes before lunch time. She could see herself in a yellow frock, her arms raised, swirling in answer to the gentle breeze that touched them playfully. Yes, she could see herself as a daffodil.

"Keira Lewis!" A voice interrupted her daydreams. "Come and write the answer to number six on the board."

Reluctantly she got up from her seat, knowing she hadn't been listening and didn't have the faintest idea what the question was let alone the answer. Several pairs of eyes regarded her sympathetically as she took the chalk from Mr Lucas's hand and tried to make some sense of the figures on the board. She knew it was something to do with angles but what she wasn't quite sure.

Screwing up her face in concentration she pretended to study the diagram.

"Well," Mr Lucas prompted. "Were you listening?"

"Mmm." Keira mumbled, wondering whether to come clean and admit that she wasn't or to try and bluff her way out.

"I know," a voice called. "It's twenty-seven degrees."

"Hopkins! Don't call out."

Keira looked round, realising she had been let off the hook. The answer was bound to be right because Colin Hopkins was the brains of the class when it came to maths and Keira guessed that he had shouted out on purpose as he could see that she was struggling. She sent him a relieved look as she returned to her seat and was sure that he winked at her. Pity he was pale, gingery and overweight with light blue eyes peering from behind National Health glasses. If he had been cute like Adam Johnson, Keira might have felt more grateful at being rescued by him.

That was one of the problems with Keira, she always had her nose in a book and thought real life should be just like a fairy tale. The second problem was that she was always dancing. She just couldn't help it. Everything made her want to dance, from the clumps of daffodils swaying outside her window to the sound of the street as she walked home at night. She found the rhythm of the cars, the revving of buses, the tinkle of bicycle bells made a fascinating symphony that her feet just couldn't resist.

She was always being told off for not standing still in line, for tapping out a tune with her spoon as she waited in the lunch queue, for hopping and skipping and jumping her way round town on a Saturday morning when she went shopping with her mother.

"Keira! For goodness sake stand still for five minutes," she was constantly being told as her mother shopped impatiently in the supermarket.

"Keira! Don't fidget." Her teachers were constantly reminding her.

"Keira! Can't you keep sit still for once?"

But it was so hard when music played, when the breeze danced in the trees or shadows drifted across the lawn in the evening. She wanted to dance with them. To twist like them and glide through the night like a moonbeam.

Wherever she was Keira wanted to dance. It was something she just couldn't help. She twisted and twirled, turned and jumped and spun. No matter how many times she was told to stop, Keira just couldn't help dancing.

And when she couldn't dance, she would read about dancing. Every book in the library had been taken out and perused by Keira. Every Saturday her friend Lucy would call for her and they would walk into town together. But, while Lucy was lucky enough to actually go to a dance class, Keira had to make do with an hour spent in the library reading everything she could about the subject.

"Why don't you come too?" Lucy had asked many times. "Ask your mum. I'm sure she will say yes when she knows how keen you are."

But no matter how many times Keira asked, pleaded even, Lauren Lewis was adamant that her daughter couldn't go to dance classes.

Eventually Keira gave up. She knew that they didn't have much money to spare; her mother had to work very hard at her job as a hairdresser to provide all the things that they needed, let alone afford dance lessons. Keira felt it was wrong to pester. Her mother looked so tired sometimes that she was spurred into offering to help; tidying her room, doing the ironing, washing up, anything to give her mum chance to put her feet up for ten minutes.

The dance lessons would have to wait, she realised that, but she didn't understand why her mother seemed so set against the whole thing. Whenever Keira wanted to dance around the house her mum would tell her to sit down and be quiet, she had a headache. When she practised gymnastics in the garden her mum would tell her to mind the plants and when she actually got a part in the school play her mum was always too busy to help her learn her words.

Keira couldn't help feeling disappointed. Not just that they couldn't afford any lessons but that her mum never showed any interest in what she wanted to do. It was as if she didn't want her to dance. Keira couldn't imagine why. What harm could there be in dancing?

Sometimes she went to Lucy's house after school. Mrs Green didn't have a problem with her daughter going to dance class. In fact, she seemed quite proud of her, displaying pictures of her in her tutu on the sideboard, trophies in the dining room and exam certificates framed in Lucy's bedroom.

Keira would look at them enviously. She loved to try on Lucy's ballet shoes, she knew how to tie the ribbons correctly, and take the frothy tutus out of the cases Lucy kept under her bed. She would sit with them in her lap and imagine what it would be like to wear them. She really would be a dancer then, twirling and gliding like a swan on a lake.

But she had to put them back, sighing heavily, when she and Lucy went downstairs for tea. The conversation around the table would revolve around Lucy's dancing, even Mr Green would join in, asking what she had done in the last ballet class and when she was taking another exam or what part she had in the next concert.

Keira had to sit and listen to all this, wishing conversations like this were normal in her house, soaking up all the information she could yet tingling with jealousy because she couldn't do anymore than sit and listen.

At night, back in her own room, she would read another chapter from her latest library book, which she kept hidden in case her mother told her off for wasting her time. Then she would fall asleep dreaming that she was on the stage, twirling and twirling in one of Lucy's tutus, a gentle flutter of snowflakes falling all around her and the applause of the audience rising in her ears.

She would curtsey graciously, acknowledging the cheers of the crowd, lowering her eyes and kissing her finger tips in a modest kind of way. The last thing she wanted was to be thought big-headed. That was something else her mother hated, so she wouldn't let fame spoil her and make her into one of those precocious children her mother thought so little of.

Neighbour's children, even relatives, were berated by Lauren Lewis for being show-offs. It was considered the eighth deadly sin and Keira knew, no matter how famous she became, she would never be like one of those "little horrors" as her mother referred to them.

Falling asleep to the sound of applause, her final vision the curtain sweeping closed before her bemused eyes, as she drifted off to sleep and, hopefully, more dreams filled with stars and moonbeams.

Chapter two

Summer was Keira's favourite time of the year. She loved it when she could wear her cotton, blue check dress for school although she was less keen on the ankle socks that went with the uniform. Secretly, she thought that her legs were too pale and skinny for ankle socks but there was the possibility that she might get some tan on her legs by the end of the summer.

She also loved the lazy feeling of lying around on the playing fields during lunch break, making daisy chains with her friends and chatting or reading. Of course she loved spending time with Lucy, Katy or Emma but to be stretched out in the sun with her latest book from the library was an even greater treat. A blade of grass sucked between her teeth made it even more enjoyable and it was always a disappointment to hear the bell ring and know she had to spend the next few hours shut inside while the day wasted away without her.

Lucy had been off school for a few days with a cold, giving Keira the chance to finish the book she had been reading since her last visit to the library. With a sigh, she turned the last page, relieved to find that the heroine finally became the star of the show, despite all the attempts of her jealous rival to stop her, and she wished that real life could be like that so she could be a dancer like she was always dreaming of.

Now the book was finished, she rested her chin between her hands and gazed across the playing field, away from the school building and into the distance where she could just make out a range of hills that she knew marked the boundary between England and Wales. Her mother came from Wales, Keira had been born there but had never been back since and it seemed to her a mysterious place inhabited by dragons and full of brooding, mist-topped mountains.

She was determined to go there one day but, whenever she suggested it to her mother, she received the silent treatment that was so characteristic of Lauren Lewis. What was the mystery that surrounded everything in her past? She wished she knew. Why was it that certain topics brought a disapproving look from her mother and left Keira with the feeling that she had done something wrong?

The school bell broke into her reverie and she was almost glad to return to the relative safety of her history lesson. History was a subject she quite enjoyed, especially when Miss White was teaching them about the Tudors, so she could spend the next hour five hundred years away from her problems. After all, she wasn't facing the possibility of beheading by a disgruntled monarch.

There was no hurry to get home at the end of the day. Lauren had her own beauty salon which meant she was quite often very late; Keira usually got her own tea when she got in, something easy like beans on toast or scrambled egg. Today she decided to call in on Lucy on her way back to see how she was. She might even get asked to stay by Mrs Green which would mean she wouldn't have to make her own. Yes, that would be a good idea.

So, she made a slight detour, turning left at the end of Church Street and heading for the large, modern house where her friend lived. Keira rang the bell, stopping to stroke Mimi who was sunning herself on the front step and admiring the neatness of the front garden as she did so.

Mr Green looked after the garden; it was his pride and joy, especially the roses that bloomed in deep hues of reds and crimson. Keira wished she had a garden like that instead of a small patch of gravel at the front of the house with one, chipped pot abandoned in the middle. Occasionally her mother planted some pansies or petunias from the garden centre but then she invariably forgot to water them so they shrivelled up and died.

Not for the first time Keira wondered what it must be like to have a father to take care of them. Someone to look after the garden, wash the car and fix things when they got broken. She envied Lucy many things and one of them was her father who always had time to spend with the two girls and was an invaluable source of information when it came to doing homework, especially maths.

It was Mrs Green who came to the door and she smiled when she saw Keira.

"Hello dear, have you come to see Lucy? She's feeling a bit better today. She could do with a visitor to cheer her up, face like a fiddle last time I went up."

Keira was never quite sure whether Mrs Green was joking or not but she was pretty sure Lucy must be really bored by now.

"I thought she might like to borrow my library book, I've finished it."

"That's very kind of you. Go on up. I will bring you some drinks up in a minute."

"Thanks, Mrs Green."

Keira skipped up the stairs and tapped on the door of Lucy's room. A voice feebly called out "hello?" but Keira was already opening the door by then and she smiled cheerfully at her friend, sprawled across the bed in her Eeyore pyjamas. Her brown hair had been plaited on either side of her head and the plaits stuck out awkwardly, making her look like a cartoon character. She looked pale and listless and Keira couldn't help feeling sorry for her. It must be horrible being ill when the weather was so nice and you couldn't go outside and enjoy it.

"I brought you a book," Keira said, perching on the edge of the bed and pulling it out of her school bag. "It's a library one so you will have to give it back."

"Thanks." Lucy didn't share Keira's great love of reading and she really wasn't up to doing much at the moment except wallowing in self pity.

Mrs Green appeared with two glasses of lemonade and fussed around for a couple of minutes, straightening pillows and tidying the duvet.

"How are you feeling?"

"I'm fine mum, really. Can't I get up yet?"

"Well, maybe tomorrow. We'll see how you feel in the morning."

Lucy sighed and scrunched back down in the freshly plumbed pillows, kicking off the duvet the minute her mother had left the room.

"Really, it's such a nuisance. She won't let me get up. I need to practise for the show. I've already missed one dance class and, if I miss another Miss Shelley won't let me be in the show and Olivia Burton will get my part instead. She always wanted to dance the part of the

12

Silver Fairy and she's probably hoping right now that I won't be back."

Keira could sympathise with her friend, she had heard all about Olivia Burton several times before and she sounded a stuck-up, thoroughly spiteful girl. She could tell how much it peeved Lucy to think that Olivia might get the role she had been practising so hard for, and all because of a stupid cold.

"I hope she doesn't get it," Keira said. "You've been practising for weeks."

"And I even have my costume," Lucy replied with a sniff. "Look, it's there, hanging behind the door."

Keira went over to look at the silver creation floating dreamily on a coat hanger.

"It's lovely," she sighed enviously, smoothing the tulle skirt of the tutu.

"You can take it down if you like. Try it on. I've got silver shoes to go with it. There, in the box."

"No, I couldn't," Keira started to say, but she had already taken the dress down and was holding it against herself, admiring herself in Lucy's full-length mirror. She twisted from side to side and watched how the skirt floated around her as she moved.

"Put it on," Lucy urged. "Then I can see what it looks like. The shoes, mask and tiara as well. You're the same size as me so it will easily fit."

Lucy had perched on the edge of the bed in her excitement and Keira needed no second bidding to try on the gorgeous dress. She had kicked off her school shoes and wriggled into the bottom half of the tutu before dropping her cardigan and dress on the floor.

"Careful," Lucy warned her, sliding off the bed to help Keira fasten the tutu with the little zip that ran up the side. "It looks great on you. Try the shoes on."

Keira knew how to tie the ribbons on ballet shoes; she had tried Lucy's on many times before, even practising some of the steps with her. They were a bit big; Lucy was a size larger than her and slightly taller too. Keira pointed her toe just like Lucy had shown her before and held her arms out in second position, her fingers held just how she had been shown so her hands were curved and not all stiff like a bird's beak.

"That's perfect," Lucy commented. "Now the mask and tiara."

Carried away by the excitement of the moment Keira slipped the silver mask across her eyes and placed the tiny, sparkling tiara in her hair.

"You look amazing."

Keira had to admit, she looked pretty good and she pulled her feet together, rising *demi-pointe* and stretching her arms above her head in fifth position.

"You look like a real ballet dancer," Lucy admitted in surprise. "No one would think that you didn't even go to ballet lessons."

"I wish I did," Keira admitted. "But mum just won't let me, I even offered to earn the money myself, do a paper round or something, but she just says it's all a waste of time."

"Not really," Lucy said. "You learn all sorts of things even if you don't ever become a ballerina. Grace, poise, stamina, all that sort of thing."

"I know. I've even tried telling her that but she's so dead against it. I don't really know why."

"Well, you can borrow my stuff whenever you like," Lucy told her generously, well aware of how lucky she was to have parents that gave her everything she wanted when it came to her dance classes. They were extremely proud of their daughter, drove her back and forth to dance classes, exams and rehearsals and were always telling everyone about their talented daughter.

"I've got an idea!" Lucy exclaimed, watching Keira twirl about in front of the mirror in her *Silver Fairy* costume. "Why don't you go to the class instead of me? That way Olivia won't get to play my part."

"Don't be silly," Keira said, stopping so suddenly that she nearly tripped over her own feet. "I wouldn't know what to do. And I would be so rubbish that Miss Shelley would give the part to Olivia straight away."

"No you wouldn't, I would show you what to do. You could wear the mask so no one would see you, with your hair tied up in a bun they won't notice your hair is blond not brown. Please, Keira. It would be easy."

"Well..." Keira knew it was a ridiculous idea; they wouldn't get away with it. There was no way she could dance like Lucy who had been having lessons for years. But still, the idea sounded fun, and it might be the only chance she ever got to dance in a proper dance class.

"Please, please, please Keira. You won't get into trouble, I promise you. Look, this is what you have to do. Third position, arms in bras bas and..."

And Keira was learning the steps for the *Silver Fairy* before she had time to argue with Lucy about it.

Chapter three

By Saturday Keira had learnt all the steps to the dance. It had proved surprisingly easy, with Lucy teaching her from her bed and Keira practising late into the night at home. It had caused her mother to come in at eleven o'clock one night to find out what the noise was and Keira had to persuade her that she had just tripped getting out of bed to get a drink of water. Her mother regarded her suspiciously, told her to be more careful, and went back to bed in a hurry.

Keira found she was so tired during the day that she nearly fell asleep once or twice during lessons but, as she always sat quietly during class, no one really noticed. She somehow managed to get her homework done, as well as the dance practise, so by the time Saturday arrived, she was surprised at how quickly it had crept up on her.

She woke up early, a vague feeling that this was not a usual Saturday, and then remembered. Today she had to pretend to be Lucy and dance the *Silver Fairy* in the rehearsal. She was struck again by how silly the whole idea was and made her mind up to tell Lucy she couldn't do it.

But Lucy was so disappointed when Keira tried to suggest it that she found herself clutching a case packed with the costume and heading for the dance school before she had chance for second thoughts. She had been to the school once or twice before, to meet Lucy on a Saturday morning so they could go into town together. She had always envied Lucy for belonging here, she walked in and out so easily, with so much confidence and now Keira stood hesitantly outside trying to build up the courage to join the throng of children going inside.

There seemed to be a great mix of ages from tiny tots to teenagers and several adults too, parents or teachers, or maybe even students. Keira wondered what it would be like to be part of this exciting community and she shivered slightly with anticipation.

Well, it was no good just standing here, she told herself, she had promised Lucy and she couldn't let her down now. With a deep breath she joined a group of children that had just arrived and followed them into the building. No one said anything to her so she tried to act as if she was meant to be there, desperately trying to remember the instructions Lucy had given her.

There was a changing room somewhere, up the stairs and to the right, but Lucy had said don't go in there because all her friends would be changing in there and they might ask questions if they saw her with the *Silver Fairy* costume. There was a *chill out* room further along the corridor, with toilets in and Lucy had told her to go in there to change. Hopefully no one would be in there so she could get changed without anyone asking what she was doing.

Keira found the room without too much trouble, partly due to the large sign with *Chill Out Room* written on it. There were two older girls in there reading magazines and drinking coke from a can, but neither looked up when she walked in so she hurried past them and straight into the ladies' loo at the far end.

It was warm in there and she put her case next to the radiator ready to change. She needed the toilet but she knew that was only nerves and she was soon wriggling into the costume, there were even silver tights to wear with it and she found these slightly uncomfortable, making her legs itch as she pulled them up. She hoped that would stop soon.

Keira realised there was a problem when she tried to do up the tutu. Lucy had always done that for her before and she couldn't reach the zip very easily. She wondered if one of the girls would help her and if she dared ask them. Well, she had no choice really. It was either that or go into the classroom undone.

"Excuse me," she whispered to the nearest girl, who seemed less engrossed in her magazine than the blond one. "Could you do my zip for me?"

The girl looked up curiously. "Who are you?"

"The *Silver Fairy*," Keira replied, almost truthfully.

"Ok, *Silver Fairy*," the girl replied laughing. "I'm Lara so I hope you will grant me three wishes."

Keira curtsied. "But of course."

She skipped back to the toilets feeling slightly more confident than she had a few minutes before; at least Lara seemed to think she should be here so she couldn't be too unbelievable.

Tying the shoes exactly how she had been shown, then arranging the mask and tiara so that most of her face and hair were hidden, she regarded herself in the mirror for a few moments before shoving her day clothes back into her case and heading back out to the corridor.

The two girls had gone and no one questioned her as she made her way downstairs to the main rehearsal room where Lucy had told her the practise would take

18

place. There were several children, boys as well as girls, moving about the place in various costumes, leotards and tutus so she didn't feel out of place. The rehearsal room was even more of a buzz with fairies of every hue, cobwebs, butterflies and even a giant caterpillar struggling into an awkward looking costume. It was like hatching in reverse and Keira couldn't help giggling at the sight.

"Don't stand there laughing," a cross voice said. "Help me with this thing, can't you?"

So Keira put down her case and tried to work out how the boy was supposed to fit into such a strange costume, with dozens of legs attached and a long zipper down the side. She helped him as best she could, only once catching the skin of his leg in the teeth of the zip. For which he let out a loud squeal and glared at her crossly.

"Be more careful," he growled and Keira started to apologise.

"Are you alright there, Michael?" Someone asked and a teacher came over to help, so Keira moved away quickly before she was asked any questions.

Finding a safe corner to hide in she stood and watched the preparations that were going on. She wondered which girl was the dreaded Olivia, but it wasn't too hard to guess. One girl stood out from all the rest, tall, slim with dark hair drawn back in a classical bun, she was dressed in a lilac tutu and was busy practising battements at the barre.

Keira watched her nervously. She could tell that she was very good and she knew there was no way she could compete with her. Why, oh why had she agreed to this mad idea?

And then she remembered, it was to help her friend. She would have to do it, and do her best, for Lucy. Keira remembered some of the exercises she had seen

Lucy do and she turned to the barre, grasping it lightly with her right hand and began to do demi-pliés. Heels together, knees bent out over her toes, back straight and head looking straight ahead. Watching Olivia she copied her carefully, toes pointed to the front, leg raised and lowered, raised and lowered, then out to the side, raised and lowered, raised and lowered, then behind, raised and lowered, raised and lowered. She even tilted her head in exactly the same way, looking into her arm as she bent it and lifted and lowered it again.

A rapid clap of hands and a scale played on the piano brought the class to attention.

"Good morning, class."

"Good morning, Miss Shelley."

"Lines please, class."

The children hastily shuffled into three neat rows and Keira wondered where she was meant to be. She noticed that the smaller ones were at the front and the tallest at the back so she manoeuvred herself into the most inconspicuous place she could find and stood in first position, her arms resting lightly by her side, just like all the other children were.

The caterpillar, otherwise known as Michael, was standing in front of her which helped to conceal her slightly, plus she remembered that she was a bit smaller than Lucy so she didn't think she would be too noticeable.

"A few stretches to warm up with, then we will practise the second act of the ballet. I see most of you are in costume, which is good. And those that aren't, please remember there is only one more week to the show. Any problems, see me at the end of the class. Now! Begin! And one and two and three and four."

Due to the limitations of some of the costumes, the warm up exercises were only basic, which was good for

Keira who was able to copy most of the steps and hide behind Michael when she was unsure what to do next. She was beginning to relax, finding that she was enjoying the class and trying her hardest to get it just right.

After fifteen minutes they were told to make space in the centre of the room for the rehearsal to begin and those that weren't in the first scene had to continue warm-up exercises so their muscles didn't stiffen up. Keira had forgotten which scene she had to dance in and stood hesitantly at the back of the room, pretending that she was tying the ribbons on her shoes and totally forgot that she was meant to be Lucy when Miss Shelley called her name several times.

"Lucy! You really aren't paying attention today. You have made one or two mistakes already this morning."

Keira was dismayed. She thought she had done rather well so far and hadn't realised that Miss Shelley had been aware of her in the back row.

"Don't think I didn't notice. Now, take your place."

Oh no. Keira knew the dance but she wasn't sure where she was meant to stand to begin with. Pretending to be straightening her tiara she walked into the centre of the room and took up the pose exactly as Lucy had shown her.

"No, no. More to the left. You are in the wings as the curtain comes up. That's it now, piano and one, two, three."

Keira danced perfectly. She remembered the story that Lucy had told her, about the spell put on the countryside by an evil queen and how the *Silver Fairy* was the only one who could save them by sprinkling her magic fairy dust on all the sleeping creatures. The music guided her, step by step, and she danced just like the fairy would have done, rescuing all the animals from the wicked spell.

As the music faded she folded her hands in front of her, pointed one toe neatly behind her ankle and bent her knee. There was a moments silence then a short ripple of applause rang out from all the children standing around the room. They had been watching her, even Olivia, although she stood with a scowl upon her face. There was no chance she would get to dance the *Silver Fairy* now.

"Well done, Lucy. Warm down now and let's have all the butterflies for the finale. Ok girls, in groups of three. Jennifer, you will have to join with Carla's group today and hope the twins are better by next week. Feet in third and..."

The piano tinkled on and Keira watched the smallest girls do their steps; running with their arms outstretched and pausing every now and then in butterfly shapes. It looked so simple. How she wished she had had dance lessons when she was that age.

A voice interrupted her thoughts. It was Michael. "You danced better than last time. Now Olivia definitely won't get the part."

Keira didn't know what to say. Did Michael mean that she had danced better than Lucy had? No, that wasn't possible. And did they all know about Olivia wanting to be the *Silver Fairy*? Keira had thought that it was only Lucy's imagination, but obviously not. So she really had saved her friend's part in the show after all. That was something to be pleased about anyway.

Now that her dance was over, Keira felt herself bubbling with excitement. She had done it, and she had done it well! She couldn't wait to tell Lucy and her friend would be so happy to know she was still to dance in the show.

The butterfly dance had come to an end. There was another short burst of applause, then Miss Shelley clapped her hands again.

"Class! Lines please. Take a curtsey."

They again formed the three lines and curtsied first to the left and then to the right, apart from Michael who, now unencumbered by his caterpillar suit, made a perfect bow.

"Thank you class. See you next week."

Excited chatter broke out as they began to make their way to the door at the back of the room. Even Michael seemed a lot happier now he was back in human form and grinned from ear to ear as he skipped out of the room.

Keira went to pick up the case she had left in the far corner.

"Just a minute, Lucy. I would like a word with you. Come here, please."

Keira froze. Oh no, what was she going to do now? She could hardly ignore the teacher but she didn't want to have to talk to her. She certainly didn't sound like Lucy.

"Well, young lady?" Miss Shelley waited; her arms folded, and regarded Keira quizzically. "Just who are you?"

Her heart sinking to her feet Keira could only hang her head, feeling a blush rising up her neck and filling her cheeks with crimson.

"I know you're not Lucy. Please take that mask off when I am talking to you. Now, let's start at the beginning shall we? Where's Lucy?"

"She's ill," Keira mumbled. "She didn't want Olivia to have her part in the show so she asked me to come today instead."

"I see. And just who are you?"

"Keira. Keira Lewis. Lucy's best friend."

"Well, I don't suppose you can take all the blame for this little escapade," Miss Shelley said, her voice softening slightly. "In fact, you danced very well. Where do you learn?"

"Lucy taught me."

"I know that. You wouldn't have known the steps for the *Silver Fairy* otherwise, seen as I choreographed them. I mean which dance school do you go to?"

"I don't. My mother won't let me. Lucy just taught me the steps so I could come today and..."

Suddenly it was all too much for Keira. The excitement of earlier, the nerves, the wonder of actually dancing a real part with people watching her. It all bubbled up and tears began spilling down her face. She could feel the mask getting wet and she tried to take it off, struggling with the elastic that got caught around the tiara.

"Wait! Let me help, I don't think Lucy wants this back damaged. Now calm down. Here, have a tissue and blow your nose."

Miss Shelley removed the mask, handing Keira a tissue and guided her by the elbow over to the piano where she sat her down on the stool.

"Now, start again, but slowly this time. Your name is Keira and you don't go to dance classes but you learnt the steps in just a week?"

"That's right," Keira sniffed, suddenly sensing that she wasn't in trouble any more. Miss Shelley didn't seem cross, more incredulous really, so Keira took a deep breath and began telling her all about being friends with Lucy, and how she envied her dance lessons because her mother wouldn't let her go. Then Lucy had been ill and asked her to take her place because she was worried about Olivia dancing the *Silver Fairy* in the show.

"I will speak to Lucy about that later," Miss Shelley said. "Meanwhile, what are we going to do about you?"

"Me?" Keira asked in surprise. She really hoped she wasn't going to get into any trouble, her mother would be furious and Lucy had promised that it would be alright.

"Yes, you. If you can learn all those steps in just a few days, and dance well enough to convince most people that you really were Lucy, then you must have talent and it seems a shame to waste it. You say your mother won't let you have classes, do you know why? Is it the cost of them?"

"I don't really know. I have asked her loads of times. I even offered to get a job and pay for them myself."

"A job?"

"Yes, a paper round or something like that. But she just gets really cross whenever I mention it and refuses to even think about it."

"Hmm. Perhaps I could have a word with her."

"I don't think that would make any difference. Lucy's mum even asked her once if I could go with her."

"Well, let me think about it." She reached across the piano and picked up a notepad and pen.

"Keira Lewis, you said. And where do you live, Keira?"

Reluctantly, Keira told Miss Shelley her address. She really didn't want her to come round and cause problems, much as she would love to have dance lessons like Lucy did.

Miss Shelley asked her a few more questions and scribbled down some notes.

"You had better run along now, Keira. Go and get changed. For your information you don't bring outside bags or shoes into this room as it damages the wooden floors. That's something Lucy would have known. She would also have known where to stand at the beginning of the dance and I noticed you struggled with some of the warm up exercises, despite being almost perfect in the *Silver Fairy* dance.

I'm not so easily fooled, you know.

You're shorter than Lucy so the costume doesn't quite fit you but it fit Lucy perfectly when she tried it on.

I have taught her for years. All dancers have their little quirks. I knew almost straight away that it wasn't Lucy dancing but I was intrigued. I wanted to know who you were and why you were taking her place."

"I'm sorry," Keira said. She liked Miss Shelley and it seemed sneaky to have tried to trick her.

"I accept your apology. I'm sure you were only trying to help your friend. Go home now and I will speak to Lucy next week. Good bye, Keira."

"Bye Miss. Thank you."

They were both left with the distinct feeling that their paths would cross again. Fairy dust had been sprinkled across both their lives at that moment.

Chapter four

"Well?" Lucy demanded, as soon as Keira walked through the door. "What happened? Did Olivia get my part?"

"No, well at least I think she didn't. Miss Shelley didn't say."

"What do you mean? Tell me! What happened?"

"Hang on a minute and I will."

Keira put the case down and perched on the end of the bed. Lucy was dressed now but had been resting in her room at her mother's insistence. She was bouncing up and down with impatience and Keira took her time trying to explain the strange events of the morning.

"It was like this, there were two girls in the *chill out* room and I asked one of them to help me fasten the zip then..."

"Did you dance the *Silver Fairy*?" Lucy interrupted her.

"Of course I did. I said I would, didn't I?"

"And what did Miss Shelley say?"

"She guessed it wasn't you dancing, she said..."

"Oh no!" Lucy looked horrified. "Did she tell you off? Am I in trouble now?"

Keira was getting fed up of Lucy interrupting her every time she tried to tell the story. She folded her arms crossly and waited for a few moments before she replied.

"No, you're not in trouble. Neither am I, I don't think. Miss Shelley was quite nice when she spoke to me, just wanted to know why I did it so I explained about Olivia. She asked me lots of questions about where I learnt to dance..."

"But you don't have dance lessons."

"I know that." Keira had had enough of Lucy by now; she just wasn't listening at all. "You are still in the show so you better hurry up and get well. I have to go home now or mum will wonder where I am. It's her weekend off and we usually do something together. I will see you later."

She was rather disgruntled that her part in the whole escapade seemed to have been ignored by Lucy. She hadn't even said thank-you!

Keira felt rather flat walking home from Lucy's house. After the nerves and excitement of the morning, and the wonderful feeling of actually dancing a proper dance, in a real costume, she now had the bounce of a burst balloon. It wasn't fair. She was just as good as Lucy, only Miss Shelley had guessed she wasn't her, so why couldn't she have lessons too? Just because her mother thought it all a waste of time.

Well, it wasn't. It was breathtaking to dance like that, all floaty and light just like a real fairy, there must be some way she could have dance classes. She just wouldn't tell her mother about it.

Perhaps that was wrong, but she wouldn't be lying. She just wouldn't say anything at all about it. And she was sure Lucy would help her, lend her an old leotard or something. She had plenty. She just needed to think of a way of paying for them.

That was exactly what Miss Shelley was thinking as she took the older girls for a tap lesson. Keira certainly had some talent, obviously she needed proper training to pull her into shape, and she definitely had some nerve to be able to pull a stunt like that. There must be some way of arranging a few dance lessons for her. Perhaps her mother could be persuaded after all.

All day was spent pondering over the problem. There were girls in her classes who would never have what it takes to be a dancer, of any sort, yet their parents had the money to pay for any amount of lessons that they wanted. Yet a child with real talent was denied the opportunity to learn. There must be something she could do.

During a brief break mid-afternoon she managed to have a few words with Mrs Bright, another of the teachers in the dance school.

"What would you do if you spotted a child with real potential but their mother didn't want them to learn to dance?"

"It depends why she doesn't want her to have lessons. Is she frightened she will hurt herself or is she worried about the cost?"

"I don't really know, that's the problem. I was thinking of going to visit the mother."

"Might make things worse," Dolly Bright said, between sips of black coffee. "I wouldn't interfere if I were you."

"You're probably right," Cathy Shelley agreed reluctantly. "It just seems such a waste. And when you think of girls like that Lottie Carmichael, thighs like a shire horse and parents who will spend a fortune on her every whim."

"Life's like that." Dolly commented with a shrug. "Off to teach the cart horses to tap dance. Stop worrying about it; it's not your problem."

But it had become Cathy's problem and she was determined to find a solution that would be suitable for all, especially little Keira who seemed quite an extraordinary child.

The 'extraordinary child' was, at that moment, being dragged round Sainsbury's by her mother. It seemed a bit of a letdown after the morning's adventure and Keira wasn't enjoying it in the least. Even the promise of a tub of strawberry ice cream in the trolley for tea later, did nothing to cheer her up.

Why, oh why couldn't she dance? What was so wrong with it? She had asked herself that question many times before but it had taken on a new urgency now that she had actually tried it. Like being offered the ice cream then having it all snatched away at the last minute. It was making her feel extremely irritable. She wanted to run up and down the aisle as fast as she could, pushing the trolley into everything that got in her way and screaming very loudly at the end.

Wouldn't everyone be shocked? It was almost funny. Keira felt a little smile struggle onto her face but she quickly bit it back. She wanted her mother to know how annoyed she was about the whole thing. But her mother didn't seem to notice. She was too busy shopping to pay much attention to Keira.

Her day off consisted of shopping, washing, ironing and cleaning the house. Much as she tried to spend quality time with her daughter, a trip round the supermarket was not her idea of a good time either.

It would be a take-away for tea, followed by ice cream and a DVD for Keira while she settled down with a glass of something nice. It was the only time she had the chance to relax. Being the only parent was not an easy job. And running the salon as well took all her energy. It was not surprising therefore, that she failed to notice Keira's low mood. Even the fact that she went straight to bed after the DVD failed to arouse her suspicions.

Even in bed Keira couldn't settle. She read a few pages of her book but felt annoyed at the ease with which the heroine became a star overnight. Life just wasn't like that.

Turning off the light she snuggled under the duvet, hugging her favourite bear to her as she tried to sleep. But the feeling of spinning and jumping as the *Silver Fairy* kept her awake long past the time she heard her mother go to bed.

A tiny tear trickled onto her pillow and she finally fell asleep as the stars twinkled silently through her window.

Chapter five

The idea came to Miss Shelley during the show the following week. The audience had already sat through the tinies trying to remember to point their toes in the same direction at the same time, a moderately good performance by the tap class, a mime by a group of seniors and were just about to watch Scott Johnson do the Highland Fling before the end of the first half.

A short interval would be followed by a comedy duet, Juliet Darcy dancing her final solo before leaving the school to go to Italia Conti, and the grand finale. This was the ballet in which most of the pupils had a short part, including the *Silver Fairy* ably danced by Lucy Green.

It was whilst watching her that Miss Shelley remembered Keira and the way she had danced after only a week. Of course! That's what she could do. Why, Keira had thought of the idea herself and, with a bit of help from Lucy, she was sure they could make it work. She couldn't wait to tell her about it.

She was so busy thinking about it that she almost forgot to take the curtain call at the end. Curtseying gracefully first right and then left, she had been on the stage herself when she was younger; she accepted the large bouquet of flowers handed to her by Juliet. Kissing her on both cheeks she led the girl by the hand to acknowledge the cheers of the crowd.

For a brief moment she remembered back to when she was that age, just about to leave home to start at the Royal Ballet School. It was all such a long time ago. She had been filled with hopes and dreams then, dreams of becoming a star, just like Juliet was. And that made her think about Keira and how she wanted her to have that chance too.

She would speak to Lucy the following week, before they broke up for summer, see if they could get something organised before the term started properly in September.

Meanwhile there were summer classes. Perhaps she could arrange for Keira to come to some of those as Lucy usually did. That would be a good start for her, the summer classes were smaller than the usual ones as many families went away on holiday, and quite often mixed ability so Keira wouldn't stand out as the odd one out quite as much as in a grade class. It was the perfect solution.

At the end of the next lesson she asked Lucy to remain behind. For some reason Lucy thought she must be in trouble, she couldn't think of any drastic mistakes during her *Silver Fairy* dance, apart from the slight wobble in her second pirouette, so she must have done something else.

"Yes Miss Shelley?"

"I wanted to ask you about your friend, Keira."

"Oh!" Lucy was relieved that she wasn't in any kind of trouble after all, then slightly miffed that Miss Shelley wanted to ask her about someone else.

"Is it true that she hadn't had any dance classes before you taught her the *Silver Fairy*?"

33

"Yes Miss Shelley. Her mum won't let her. Thinks it's a complete waste of time and a lot of showing off."

"That's a great shame. Ballet involves a great deal of skill, dedication and talent. I think Keira has all that and I would like the chance to prove it. Do you think Keira would like to have lessons with you?"

"Yes, I'm sure she would. But her mum won't waste money on lessons; I've heard her say so."

"Let me worry about the money. You bring Keira along with you next week and we'll have a little talk about it. Do you think you could do that?"

"Of course Miss Shelley."

Lucy knew she could, but did she want to? She wasn't sure she liked the idea of her friend getting all the attention. But then, she had helped her when she thought Olivia would get her part in the show. It was only fair that she did something to help Keira now.

And there was no way Keira would be as good as her at ballet, why she'd been doing it for years. Ever since she was a tiny in a pink frock and pigtails. There was really no reason for her to be jealous of Keira; it should be the other way round.

She would bring Keira along to the next class, if that's what Miss Shelley wanted, she would even lend her some of her old shoes. It might be fun to have a friend in the class with her instead of some of the annoying younger ones who couldn't even plié properly. And she would be able to show her what to do.

Lucy brightened visibly at that thought. Keira would soon realise how good she was and how hard it was to be a good dancer.

"I will bring Keira next week," she promised. "I 'spect she'll be really pleased."

Keira was more than pleased when Lucy started to explain Miss Shelley's plan to her.

"Do you think it will work?" She exclaimed.

"Well, you've done it once already. And this time you will have help."

"And I won't need to lie; I will just say I am with you. Mum won't mind, she doesn't like me being on my own during the school holidays. She will think your mum is keeping her eye on us."

"That's great then. I've got plenty of things you can borrow so you won't need to buy anything and Miss Shelley said she would work something out about the money so you don't need to worry about that either."

Keira couldn't believe it. After all these years she was finally to have proper dancing lessons, and with the lovely Miss Shelley. It was a dream come true.

The first lesson was on Tuesday morning at ten. Keira walked to Lucy's house on a cloud, it really was true what people said about walking on air. She could hardly feel the pavement beneath her feet as she made her way along the busy road to Lucy's house.

Her excitement was infectious and Lucy could remember her first ballet lessons, she had been much younger than Keira was, obviously, but she still had the same tickling feeling in her stomach then as she suspected her friend did now.

She had already sorted out a case for Keira to take, filled with everything she could possibly need. And the two girls ran giggling from the house before Mrs Green could wonder what on earth was going on. They skipped along the High Street together and paused outside the dance school to get their breath.

The last time Keira had waited here she had been anxious in case her real identity was discovered. Now she could walk quite boldly through the front door with Lucy, smiling at the other girls who were loitering on the front steps, chatting in the corridor or warming up in the changing rooms. This time she didn't have to get changed in the toilet, she could sit with all the other girls who were getting ready for their classes and listen to their conversations, all revolving around dance classes.

Keira found it all fascinating. It was like another world. Words she had only read in books or sometimes heard from Lucy, were now being bandied around as easily as some people discussed the weather.

"Did you see Juliet in the show? Weren't her pirouettes just perfect?"

"I wish I could do entrechats like Emily Watson, she makes me green with envy."

"Lottie Carmichael is getting huge. Did you see her jétès in the last class? Like a bowl of jelly."

There were sniggers after this remark and Keira couldn't help feeling sorry for poor Lottie while making a mental note not to get too huge to be able to jété.

She changed quickly then sat on the bench and absorbed the atmosphere of the changing room. Lucy was talking to a curly-haired girl who was trying to pull her hair back into some kind of a bun and seemed to be having difficulties. Keira was glad she didn't have curly hair. Her blond hair was long and straight and she found it quite easy to twist it round the 'donut' the way Lucy had shown her and spear it with an army of grips.

The chatter all around her was high-pitched and excited. There was a peculiar smell of leather, hairspray and perspiration that could only be found in a dance changing rooms and she took a deep breath, trying to take in everything that was so new to her.

All at once the girls jumped up and started to leave the room, pulling leotards into shape and patting hair into place.

"Come on," Lucy said, and Keira followed her eagerly into a studio on the ground floor.

It was similar to the last room she had been in but smaller. It had mirrors all the way around and a barre fixed to the walls. A piano in one corner where Miss Shelley was discussing music with the pianist, a grey-haired lady in a very baggy purple sweater. She wore a purple scarf tied loosely round her head and was wearing large, dark-rimmed glasses. She appeared to be listening intently as Miss Shelley went through the routine of the class with her, nodding ever so slightly now and then.

Most of the girls went straight to the barre and began warming up. Keira watched them, keen to see everything that was going on. Lucy had found a place near the back of the room and Keira stood behind her, trying to turn her feet out in the way she knew you did for ballet.

It was strange seeing yourself reflected all around but the other girls didn't seem to notice. Nor did they pay any attention to the new girl in their midst, they were too busy trying to capture the illusive dream of perfection that each of them sought.

Miss Shelley clapped her hands.

"Lines, girls," she called, and the class formed themselves into three straight lines with the minimum of fuss and total concentration.

"Good morning, girls."

"Good morning, Miss Shelley."

Keira joined in the familiar routine with a feeling of anticipation. Then the class began. She tried her best to follow what everyone else did, listened carefully to the instructions given by Miss Shelley but still couldn't help feeling like she was the odd one out.

Every now and then Miss Shelley would come over and stand beside her, gently moving an arm or a leg, tilting her head slightly to one side or the other, but Keira didn't mind that. And she did it to the other girls too so it didn't worry her too much.

By the end of the lesson Keira ached in every muscle of her body, even parts she didn't know she had were heavy with fatigue and she longed to lie down somewhere and rest her tired feet.

A couple of the girls hung back because they wanted to speak to Miss Shelley.

"Lucy Green," Miss Shelley called. "Could I have a word with you and Keira, please?"

The two girls exchanged glances and waited nervously by the piano where Mrs Grace was sorting her sheets of music out ready for the next class. She peered at the girls over the top of her glasses but couldn't name them out of all the pink-clad figures that flitted around behind her piano.

Miss Shelley dealt briefly with the girls who had queries about lessons or wanted to inform her they would be on holiday for the next two weeks and would see her when they got back.

Finally she turned to Lucy and Keira, by which time the next class was starting to arrive. They were warming up on the barre.

"Well, how did you find it? Did you enjoy it?"

"Oh yes," Keira breathed. "It was wonderful, but I ache everywhere."

"That's because you are not used to moving in the way you do for ballet. You have to turn out from the hip, which is not the way you would stand normally. I suggest you practice the five positions, pliés and battements for half an hour every day. Are you coming back next week?"

"Oh yes, yes please."

"That's good. And Lucy, keep up the good work. Practice, practice, practice."

"Yes, Miss Shelley," both girls chorused, then skipped out of the room together.

"That was amazing," Keira burst out, unable to stand still as the adrenalin pumped through her body. She wanted to keep on dancing, spinning, jumping and twirling all the way home but had to calm down once they were back in Lucy's house.

Mrs Green asked the girls what they wanted for lunch and raised her eyebrows understandingly at their giggling and silliness. It was good to see them laughing, she often thought that Keira was too serious for her age and she wondered what had cheered her up so much today.

Before she had time to ask both girls had escaped upstairs where they spent the afternoon practicing everything they had done in the class that day. Keira thought it was one of the best days of her life.

Chapter six

The summer was a dream for Keira. Every Tuesday she went for ballet lessons with Lucy, for two hours every Wednesday morning she helped Miss Shelley with the tinies and on Thursday afternoon she had a special class with Lucy and another girl called Ellie. In this class they learnt the steps for dances, including the *Silver Fairy* which Keira now thought of as her dance.

It seemed that the school would be putting on another show at Christmas and Miss Shelley wanted each of them to dance a solo, including Keira. All three girls had to learn the steps to all the dances, just to be on the safe side, as Miss Shelley put it.

Keira pushed the thought of the show to the back of her mind, she knew it was all part of Miss Shelley's grand plan but, for now; she was just enjoying the classes and the chance to belong to the magical world of ballet. At night she dreamed about dancing and every spare moment of the day she practiced, apart from when her mother was around. Then she tried to act as if nothing was different but it was very hard.

It was hard to walk round Sainsbury's when she wanted to skip everywhere; it was hard to watch DVDs when she wanted to be in her room reading her latest book from the library. She had even become fussy about what she ate, aware that dancers couldn't put on too much weight and having to cut down on some of her favourite food such as pizzas.

Her mother gave her a funny look when she refused dessert for the second day in the row and asked if she was feeling alright.

"I'm fine, just watching what I eat."

"You're not on any silly fad diet are you?"

"No mum, I promise. I just don't want to get fat."

"That's good," Lauren agreed, stopping as she was just about to take a second spoonful of ice cream and putting the lid back on the tub.

"Perhaps you should take up a sport," she suggested.

"I've been thinking about that. I might go swimming with Lucy; it's supposed to be good exercise."

"Yes, that's fine. You've got your school swimming costume."

"Yes, but I could do with a new one, it's getting a bit tight."

"Well, we'll see."

Keira knew, without being told, that it was the money thing again so she didn't say anything. Of course, she wouldn't mention the dance classes; they would carry on being a secret for now. She knew it was the best way.

She didn't even mind when they went back to school. The lessons carried on except at a different time, Tuesday evenings and Saturday mornings. If her mother wondered why she spent so much time with Lucy she didn't ask, just glad that Keira seemed so much happier these days.

And Keira was, now that she was able to dance, she was happier than she had ever been in her life.

Plan A was progressing smoothly. Keira was learning the *Silver Fairy* under Miss Shelley's critical eye. She was also learning all the basic ballet steps she had missed out on and it was obvious she had a natural aptitude for dance. Miss Shelley only had to show her once and she could do it much to the disconcertion of Lucy who had been doing ballet all her life.

There were times when she was tempted to feel jealous but Keira never acted in a big-headed way, only eager to learn everything she could and grateful for the chance to dance, so Lucy was quite happy to help her when she could.

Both girls practised together after school and Lucy didn't mind lending Keira everything she needed for the lessons. She knew her mum didn't want her to have lessons so it all had to be kept a secret. But quite how Plan B was going to work neither of them knew.

Miss Shelley explained her idea to them and Keira looked at her in horror.

"But my mum would never come to a ballet show," she told Miss Shelley. "She hates ballet and she will go mad if she finds out I have been having lessons."

"Don't worry. I have an idea. Leave it all to me."

Keira tried not to worry about it; she just concentrated on having a good time and enjoying her dancing. She knew there was going to be another show before Christmas but she didn't mind that she wouldn't be in it; it had been more than a dream just being able to come to classes for the last few weeks.

She did feel a slight tinge of envy as she watched the others begin to practice, chatting eagerly about the part they were to play and the costumes they would be wearing. Keira noticed Lucy deep in discussion with Miss Shelley and she pretended she didn't mind. Lucy was Mrs Tiggywinks in the Beatrix Potter ballet and she was really looking forward to it. Miss Shelley told Keira to carry on practicing the *Silver Fairy* and to concentrate on the five positions of feet and arms that she had been taught. These were the basis of all ballet positions and had to be perfect before anything else could be learnt.

So Keira practiced faithfully every day. She practised pliés, porte de bras and battement tendues and worked on the *Silver Fairy*, even adding little touches of her own which Miss Shelley thoroughly approved of.

As Christmas approached the dance school grew busier and busier. There were costumes to fit and many mothers were brought in to help. Dress rehearsals, make-up lessons and practicing with hair styles, wigs and tiaras, there was never a moment to spare as the show drew closer and closer.

Then there were exams coming up at school which meant extra homework and revision and Lauren was busy too as the party season was just beginning and everyone wanted their hair or nails done and the salon was open longer hours than usual.

Keira rarely saw her mother, sometimes she didn't get home until nine o'clock at night, by which time Keira was usually in bed reading a book. Her mum would pop her head around the bedroom door and wish Keira good-night before sticking a meal in the microwave, having a shower and sitting down in front of the TV with a large glass of wine.

Even the weekends were a constant rush, Sainsbury's was a nightmare of pre-Christmas hustle and bustle and Keira dreaded it. Her mother was tired and snappy and they were both glad to get home and shut the door on the 'season of goodwill.'

Keira was starting to feel exhausted from dance classes, revision and the pressure of exams. Luckily, her mother was too busy herself to notice that Keira was paler and more out of sorts than usual. She was too excited to eat properly so skipped most of her meals, unless she was at Lucy's house when Mrs Green would insist that she joined them for tea, which she did.

The show was to be on the Saturday two weeks before Christmas and it was at the dress rehearsal that Miss Shelley revealed Part B of her plan to Keira. Keira was wearily trying to round up a dozen tinies dressed as rabbits who were more interested in pulling each others tails than in standing in a straight line. As the music started for their dance Keira felt a hand on her shoulder and turned to find Miss Shelley behind her.

"Well done, Keira," she said with a smile. "You have done really well with the tinies; we wouldn't have managed without you these last few weeks."

"That's ok," Keira replied. "I've really enjoyed it."

"I have one more favour to ask of you. I want you to dance the *Silver Fairy* in the Christmas Show."

Seeing that Keira was about to protest she held up her hand to stop her.

"Whatever you're about to say, don't. I have watched you learn the steps, I have seen how you have improved since starting lessons here and I really think you can do this. Lucy will lend you the costume."

Then it dawned on Keira that Miss Shelley had had this planned all along. What's more, Lucy must have known about it too, that's what they had been discussing so avidly the other day, she was only surprised that Lucy had managed to keep it a secret for so long.

But then, she had been busy too. The two girls had hardly seen each other all week.

"It's all worked out. The *Silver Fairy* will be the first act in the second half, that will give you time to get

44

changed during the interval. Don't argue, it's all sorted."

"Yes Miss Shelley," Keira said.

She knew she was defeated and she actually quite liked the idea. After all the hard work it would actually be good to take part in the show. And her mother would never know, she would just say she was going out with Lucy for the day. Her mother would probably be working anyway.

As the idea started to sink in she felt her excitement rising. She was actually going to dance in a show in front of a real audience. Moments of panic were interspersed with explosions of joy as she realised she was now part of all that was going on, a performer not an outsider, a dancer not just an on-looker. She didn't think life could get any better.

As they walked home together the two girls giggled over the news. Keira tried on the *Silver Fairy* costume in Lucy's bedroom and this time it looked entirely different on her, this time it was *her* costume. She twisted and turned in front of the mirror and practised the steps watching how the tutu twirled with her. In two weeks time she would be the *Silver Fairy*, in front of all the parents, relatives and friends of the ballet school children.

Apart from her own of course, the one person she longed to see her dance wouldn't be there because her mother would be angry with her for dancing. The thought was like a pin in a balloon and she paused in front of the mirror, a worried frown on her face.

"You're thinking about your mum, aren't you?" Lucy asked.

"Yes. I wish she could be there. I wish she didn't hate me dancing so much. What can be wrong with it?"

"I don't know. My parents have always been pleased that I have something I am interested in. And I am quite good at it," she added modestly.

"You're really good, Lucy. I wish I could dance like you."

"You haven't been learning as long as me. But Miss Shelley thinks you're really good."

"Really?" Keira was surprised.

"Of course. Why else would she be doing all this?"

"I don't know." Keira hadn't thought about it too much. She was just glad she had the chance to learn, she hadn't really thought about anything else but she was quite pleased to hear that Miss Shelley thought she was quite good at dancing. She loved it so much she always wanted to do her best. And she would do her best in the show as a way of saying thank you to her teacher.

At last, exams were over and the concert was drawing ever nearer. It was all Lucy and Keira could talk about. They were both equally excited about their parts and it would be the first time Keira had ever danced in front of an audience. Lucy, of course, was used to it but her friend's enthusiasm was rubbing off on her, making her feel just as nervous as if it was her first time too.

"What if I forget the steps?" Keira asked.

"You won't. Once you start the music tells you what to do. I never have and I don't remember anyone else doing. Apart from the tinies and nobody minds that. They just think they are so cute so it doesn't matter."

Keira's one consellation was that very few people in the audience would know her, apart from Lucy's parents, so it wouldn't matter too much if she did forget a step or two. Only Miss Shelley and Lucy would know.

Saturday morning dawned bright and cold. As soon as Keira woke she jumped out of bed and looked out of the window as there had been threats of snow on the weather forecast and she didn't want there to be any difficulty getting to the show. The actual performance was taking place in a real theatre but the practice would be in the dance school at various times of day. Keira and Lucy had to be there at eleven then they were going back to Lucy's house for dinner and her parents were taking them to the theatre in the evening.

Luckily, Keira's mum would be working all day in the salon so was quite pleased that she would be spending the day with Lucy as it stopped her having to worry about her.

Excitement had risen to fever pitch by the time the two girls arrived at the dance school. Exhausted tinies were leaving as their practise had been held first, giving them time to go home and rest before the evening's performance. Several of them now recognised Keira as she had helped out in their class during the holidays so they waved madly or hid shyly behind their mothers, depending on their inclination.

Keira now thought nothing of entering the dance school, making her way along the busy corridor and changing with all the other girls before the class. She was part of the whole scene now and even smiled at some of the girls she had come to know.

They changed into their practice clothes then made their way into the main classroom for their warm ups and exercises. The familiar music and routines helped to soothe their overwrought nerves and they were soon concentrating on their turn-outs and line and carriage.

Keira loved every minute of the class. She never found the exercises boring or the repetition dull. Every time she did something she tried to make it better than last time, the toes more pointed, the arm more stretched, each jump a little bit higher and the landing that bit more graceful. When they learnt something new she concentrated with every ounce of her being to understand what it was Miss Shelley wanted from her before she even attempted the step. Then she tried the movement, letting it absorb into her with the music. It all became one, Keira, the music and the step were inseparable and she was able to perform it without consciously thinking about it.

That was how she learnt to dance. And tonight was the ultimate test as people were actually going to watch her. It was terrifying and exhilarating all at the same time. For a moment she wished her mum could be there, pleased for her like Lucy's parents, and all the other parents, were pleased and proud of their children. But she knew that was impossible because her mum had such a bee in her bonnet about the whole dance thing.

And even more impossible, it was one of those moments that Keira wished she had a dad that would be there too. But that was another of her mother's 'bees.' All mention of her father was forbidden and Keira didn't know why.

Still, now was not the time to dwell on these things. She had to put all distractions behind her and concentrate on tonight's performance. Her first and maybe her last, how long she could go on having lessons in secret she didn't know.

That was another thing not to worry about. Tonight she was going to be the *Silver Fairy*, not Keira Leone Lewis, and that was all that mattered.

Chapter seven

The day had been hectic just as Lauren Lewis knew it would be. People getting ready for office parties and family gatherings all wanted their hair doing, their nails, their make-up so she didn't finally leave the salon until six-thirty.

She drove home through the drizzle that wasn't quite sleet and was surprised to find the house all in darkness as she pulled up outside. Then she remembered, Keira was spending the day with her friend. Well, it had stopped her being on her own but it did make the house seem cold and unwelcoming as she switched on the gas fire, the television and the kettle one after the other and closed the curtains to keep out the night.

She was just making herself a cup of coffee and some toast when the phone rang.

Who on earth was that? Her first instinct was it must be bad news, there had been an accident, something had happened to Keira, and she picked the receiver up with some trepidation.

A strange voice enquired if she was Mrs Lewis and she listened for some moments to the strange message that made little or no sense to her. Who was this Miss Shelley? What was she on about? Theatre? Keira? There must be some mistake.

She hung up in annoyance. She'd had nothing to eat since two o'clock and was feeling somewhat light-headed. The toaster popped up and she spread marmite still trying to work out what the telephone conversation meant.

Burning her lips on the scalding coffee she made her way into the living room where she sat in front of the television for ten minutes trying to watch the news and eat her toast.

Spending all day getting everyone else ready for Christmas she had no time to get ready herself. Her hair needed washing; she had bundled it up in some kind of a twist and held it in place with a very ragged scrunchy. Her make-up had rubbed off during the day and her work clothes were now feeling scruffy and decidedly wrinkled.

The last thing she wanted to do was go out again and make her way across town in this weather to a theatre she only vaguely knew existed all because of a mysterious telephone call. But the woman had been most insistent. And what did it all have to do with Keira?

With a reluctant sigh Lauren knew she wasn't going to be sliding into the bath she had been dreaming about all day. She would finish her coffee in a few scalding gulps, put her coat back on, go out in this horrible weather and drive to the other side of the town to find out exactly what was going on and what on earth her daughter had been up to.

A cold knot of fear tied itself in Lauren's stomach as she hurried up the steps at the front of the imposing, but slightly grubby facade, of the old building. Theatres were part of her past. They belonged to a time she had tried to escape from, to bury the memories that were now flooding back as she entered the crowded foyer and pushed her way through the throng of people chattering quite happily, buying programmes and perusing them with interest.

She had failed to read the billing outside the theatre due to the heavy rain that obscured her vision and made her want to rush inside as fast as possible. She did, however, register that there were a lot of children standing around and guessed that the performance was aimed at them. Did Keira want her to watch a show? If so, why not just say so instead of all this high-drama stuff. But then, that was just like Keira, couldn't do anything in a straightforward way.

Just as the houselights dimmed, indicating that the performance was about to begin, a hand touched her tentatively on the arm.

"Mrs Lewis? Come with me please."

Just what was all this mystery for?

Following the strange woman she found herself entering the theatre just as the conductor raised the baton and the final whisper of voices died away.

"Here. You can sit here."

The woman whispered and Lauren found herself too weary to argue, at least it was warm and dry in the theatre and she hadn't had to pay for the ticket. The worst that could happen was that she might fall asleep for a couple of hours but that wouldn't be a bad thing. After the day she'd had she was exhausted and could do with a bath but a couple more hours wouldn't make any difference. She just wished she knew what was going on.

The music began and a troupe of little girls dressed as rabbits began to hop around the stage, not all at the same time or in the same direction. No one seemed to mind and Lauren had already worked out that this was a children's show but she had no idea why she had been summoned here or what she was supposed to do now.

Several more acts followed, some better than others and she may even have enjoyed it if she didn't feel like she had been brought here under false pretences.

Thankfully, the interval arrived and she had managed to stay awake. Perhaps she could manage to sneak out now and be home in time for that hot shower she had been promising herself all day. She was just thinking about putting her coat on when the mysterious woman appeared in front of her again.

This time she was able to get a better look at her and realised she was not as young as she first appeared, maybe in her early thirties, with her hair bleached blond and a great deal too much make-up on. But that was what they were like, these theatrical types, always went over the top with everything.

"Enjoying the show?" The woman asked.

Not waiting for a reply she thrust a programme into Lauren's hands and disappeared again into the milling throng. Lauren was beginning to think she was some kind of phantom as she took the programme automatically and found herself still sitting in her seat as the lights dimmed again.

Lauren flicked through the pages, reading briefly it was a dance school production and recognising the woman in the picture as the one who had just spoken to her. She managed to read through the cast and the mystery was solved. Of course, Lucy Green. That was Keira's friend. She was in the show so Keira must have wanted her to come and watch. Though why she didn't just say so, it would have been so much easier.

As usual Lauren would have made some excuses and said she couldn't come. Was that why Keira had resorted to subterfuge? And why was it so desperately important for her to watch Lucy dance? Was it Keira's way of trying to persuade her mother to let her have dance lessons again? If so it wouldn't work, Lauren had always been adamant that her daughter would have nothing to do with ballet or the stage or anything to do with it. She was not going to follow in unsuitable footsteps.

The lights had dimmed. The music began. The curtains began to rise slowly to reveal a mysterious woodland setting with wintry branches reaching out and a moon half-hidden behind dark clouds. Lauren was intrigued; it was very different from all the previous sets. The programme had just said the *Silver Fairy* and there was no name beside it to reveal the identity of the dancer.

A young girl, clad in a very simple silver tutu, a mask covering her face and a tiara sparkling in her hair, floated onto the stage and paused dramatically in a single spotlight.

A shiver ran down Lauren's neck and she wondered why. There was something familiar about the girl but she couldn't think what. Maybe it was Keira's friend, she had seen her once or twice so that might be it. There was something compelling about the dancer. All eyes in the theatre were fixed on her, sweet packets were no longer rustling and restless children settled back in their seats as the whimsical figure drifted across the stage.

For some reason Lauren felt tears prick the back of her eyes and she blinked angrily. She wanted to leave, she had wasted enough time this evening, but something held her in her seat and she couldn't take her eyes from the silver figure until the last note had faded from the violins and the curtains came down with a heavy swish. Then a ripple of applause spread through the theatre quickly reaching a crescendo as adults and children alike showed their approval for the *Silver Fairy*.

The finale of the show featured most of the children from the dance school, even a rather large caterpillar wriggled his way across the stage at one point, but the *Silver Fairy* did not put in another appearance, much to everyone's disappointment.

When the curtain fell at the end of the performance all the children re-appeared to take a bow, except the *Silver Fairy* who had already changed out of her costume and back into the jeans and T-shirt she wore for most of the time.

"Well done, Keira," Miss Shelley whispered. "You did really well. I think everyone else thought so too."

"Thank you."

The dressing room was beginning to fill with excited children, their voices raised as they discussed their performance. Michael wriggled out of his caterpillar costume and squealed loudly as Lottie stood rather heavily on his hand.

"Watch where you're going!"

"Sorry," but she didn't sound it. She was much too busy showing her friend the arabesque she had held longer than she had in rehearsals.

"Look at my line, perfect don't you think?"

Her friend, busy untying her ballet shoes, was less than enthusiastic and wished Lottie would stop showing off. Everyone knew she was the worst dancer in the class.

Keira was waiting for Lucy. She helped her unfasten her costume and folded it carefully while Lucy shrugged into blue trousers and a pale blue sweater with snowflakes across the front.

"You did really well," she told Keira. "I expect your mum will be really proud of you. She's bound to let you have lessons now."

"My mum?" Keira grew pale under the make-up she was still wearing.

"Yes. Didn't Miss Shelley tell you? She invited your mum here to watch you dance."

"Oh no, she'll go mad."

"I'm sure she won't, now that she's seen how good you are."

"But you don't understand, she really hates anything to do with ballet. And now she will know I've been having lessons behind her back."

To Lucy it was incomprehensible that any mother wouldn't be pleased with their daughter's wonderful performance, such as Keira had danced tonight. She was sure Keira must be exaggerating.

Some of the older performers, now changed, were leaving the room to find their parents and some of the tinies' mothers had made their way into the changing room to help their exhausted offspring out of their costumes and into their outdoor clothes.

Lucy hung her costume up on the rails and put on her boots and coat ready to find her parents. They would be waiting in the foyer as they usually did. Keira followed her nervously, hoping it wasn't true about her mother being there.

"Keira!" A voice called across the din.

Lucy raised her eyebrows sympathetically and hurried over to where her parents were waiting. Keira saw her being enveloped in a hearty hug as she made her way reluctantly to where her mother was waiting. She didn't look very pleased.

"What are you doing here?"

"I should be asking you that question. I just can't believe it, after all I've said to you."

There was no use trying to deny it. Keira's hair was still drawn up in a classical bun and she knew there were traces of make-up on her face even though she had tried to wipe it off with a tissue. The type of make-up they wore on stage didn't come off very easily and she still had silver glitter on her face from the mask that she had worn.

"I just don't know what to say to you."

Lauren had Keira by the shoulder and she was already steering her towards the door, through the crowds who were excitedly discussing the show. From the corner of her eye she saw Michael with his family; they were happy and laughing as he tried to demonstrate a particularly tricky step.

Keira wished her mother was happy and laughing, or hugging her warmly like Lucy's mum or smiling broadly like Lottie's parents were. But her mother had a dark frown on her face and Keira felt her heart sink as they stepped outside into the street.

Groups were still clustered on the pavement, despite the cold and snowflakes that were beginning to fall. They didn't seem to want to go home, hanging onto the magic of the theatre for as long as possible.

For Keira the magic vanished very quickly as they made their way to the car park in silence. She stuffed her hands deeper into her pockets and hurried across to the car. She was just about to speak when her mother started up the engine, drowning out the sound of her voice.

"You will go straight to your room when we get home," her mother instructed. "And one thing's for sure, there'll be no more dancing."

Chapter eight

Keira woke with a strange feeling in her chest and aching legs. As she remembered that her legs were aching because of the show last night she also realised that the heavy feeling in her chest was disappointment. Her mother had seen her dance and forbidden her to have lessons ever again.

Miss Shelley's plan had failed. Keira desperately wished that she hadn't told her mother about it but she was only doing what she thought was best. Miss Shelley hadn't realised just how much her mother hated all that "showing off" as her mother often referred to ballet. Although why she thought like that was a mystery to Keira.

She turned over in bed and picked up the book she had been reading the night before. Suddenly she didn't have the heart to go on with it. Of course the girl in the story would go on to become a famous ballerina, despite the opposition of her jealous arch-rival, Amanda. If only real life was so easy.

Her mother would have hugged her last night, told her how proud she was of her and that she would do anything to see her only child reach her dream. Instead she had sent her to her room and refused to discuss the matter further.

A warm tear trickled down Keira's face and she dropped the book back onto the floor. She couldn't bear to read it. Veronica would become a ballerina but Keira wouldn't and it was her own mother who was stopping her. It just didn't seem right somehow.

As more tears started to fall she heard her mother stirring in her room next door. She heard the curtains opening, then the door as her mother went into the bathroom. She could hear water starting to run, her mum always had a bath on a Sunday morning, she said it was her treat after a busy Saturday in the salon. And Keira would usually go downstairs and get the breakfast ready so they could sit together and have toast, orange juice and coffee for her mum and chat about their plans for the day.

Today Keira didn't feel like getting up. She couldn't face her mother and certainly didn't want to talk about her plans that were all in ruins anyway. She would pretend she was asleep, tired out from last night's show and would stay in bed until lunch time. Longer if she could, she would pretend she was sick and stay in bed all day.

Or maybe that wasn't a good idea. Would her mother say that's what comes of dancing? It would give her another reason for stopping her going to classes. Well, she certainly wasn't going to get up and make breakfast. She wasn't hungry anyway and her mum could get her own. Her mother was her least favourite person just at the moment.

It was easy to drift off again. She really was tired after her late night and in her dreams she was once again the *Silver Fairy*. This time, as she took a curtain call, the audience rose and cheered, Miss Shelley presented her with an enormous bouquet and her mother cheered loudest of all.

Smiling, waving and blowing kisses gracefully with the tips of her fingers Keira acknowledged the crowd. The cheers grew louder and louder, someone was calling her name.

"Keira. Keira! KEIRA!"

With a start she realised that her mother was calling her and the cheers were actually her knocking on the bedroom door.

"Do you know what time it is? Get up. Breakfast is ready."

Opening her eyes Keira glanced at the clock beside her bed. It was half past ten. Reluctantly she dragged herself out of the bed and into the bathroom. She supposed she would have to face her mother eventually; she couldn't stay in bed for ever.

At least she had another week at school before the Christmas holidays so there was only today to get through before she was out of her mother's way. And she knew her mother would be very busy in the salon the final week before Christmas. Perhaps she would be so busy she would forget all about Keira and the dancing lessons.

Her mother was drinking coffee and flicking through a beauty magazine as if nothing unusual had happened. Keira made herself some toast and poured a glass of orange juice. Nervously she sat opposite her mother, hoping to avoid any conversation with her. But her mother was engrossed in the magazine, or at least she appeared to be, perhaps she was pretending too.

Keira really didn't have much appetite for breakfast but she nibbled a slice of toast and swallowed the juice as quickly as she could. Then she went to the sink to wash up, glad to have something to concentrate on and taking as long as possible to wash the plates and cutlery so she could appear too busy to speak to her mother.

Then she dried them and put them away before escaping into the living room to switch on the TV and fill the silence that seemed to be pervading the house.

She found the children's channel, she wouldn't normally watch it but it distracted her from the thoughts she didn't want irritating her and she really couldn't be bothered doing anything else at the moment. Normally she would do her homework but there was none with it being the last week of term, and her mother would sit in the kitchen and do the accounts for the salon.

At least it kept them apart for a while. Keira just couldn't think what she would say to her when they finally came face to face. Curled up in the corner of the sofa was a good place to be right now.

By twelve she was starting to feel peckish but she couldn't pop into the kitchen for a biscuit or some fruit like she normally did. Her mum would be there, she would just have to wait until lunch time.

Her stomach was beginning to rumble by the time she heard pots and pans being rattled in the kitchen and she was quite relieved when she heard her mother call her name this time, it meant lunch was ready.

Springing from the sofa she was half way across the room before she remembered the disagreement with her mother and entered the kitchen silently. Her mother was serving vegetables onto plates as Keira slipped into her usual seat by the window.

"Is that enough?"

"Yes thanks."

Keira poured herself a glass of water and nibbled at her food. Under the watchful eye of her mother she had suddenly lost her appetite again. It was her favourite, roast chicken, roast potatoes, carrots and peas but she picked her way through it leaving most of it on her plate. Her mother said nothing as she cleared the plates away and placed a bowl of apple crumble and custard in front of Keira.

Well, that would have been really hard to resist but she didn't scrape it up with her usual gusto. She washed up silently as her mother drank a cup of coffee and pretended she was listening to a play on the radio.

The silence was heavier than the custard they had eaten and neither of them was happy with it but didn't know how to break it. It was very rare that the two of them fell out and it was not a pleasant feeling.

"What are you up to for the rest of the day?"

"Don't know. Might read in my room."

"No homework?"

"Not this week."

"Soon be Christmas."

"Yes."

Keira was no longer looking forward to it. It was as if Santa himself had suddenly said he didn't believe in Christmas. The magic had all disappeared. The *Silver Fairy* had all been a figment of her imagination and it had been waved away with a touch of her mother's wand.

There were no dreams now, nothing to look forward to or hope for. It had been nice while it lasted but it was over now. She would never be allowed to dance again. Tears began to well up in her eyes so she hurriedly left the room. The last thing she wanted was for her mother to see her cry. She would shut herself up in her room until tea time, like Rapunzel in the tower she would wait for the spell to be broken.

But there was no handsome prince to rescue her, no fairy godmother to tell her she could go to the ball after all. And Keira lay on her bed and cried.

Chapter nine

The last week of term was usually full of excitement but Keira just couldn't get into the spirit of things. There were no proper lessons, just quizzes and lots of tidying up. She always thought it was a shame that they had to take the decorations down before Christmas. The classrooms were bare and empty and only the hall remained decorated ready for the Christmas party that was held on the last day.

Keira did manage to feel a bit more in the party spirit as she changed into her best dress on Friday lunchtime. It was hard not to catch the excitement that was buzzing round the girls' changing rooms as they each admired each other's frocks and shoes, helped with hair and even an occasional touch of make-up.

Some of the girls looked quite grown up and Keira felt a bit silly in her blue velvet party dress. She brushed her long hair but preferred it down whereas a few of them, including Lucy, were putting theirs up.

"Can you help me?" Lucy asked impatiently. "I want this grip in the back so I can put my hair up."

"Of course." Keira tried to follow the instructions she was being given but she was all fingers and thumbs and she kept snagging Lucy's hair.

"Oww! Are you doing it on purpose?"

"Of course not. Keep still."

"I am keeping still. Oh, forget it. I will get Harriet to do it. Harri, can you give me a hand please?"

"Sure, what do you want?"

Harriet had Lucy's hair up in a few swift twists and secured it with the grip she had been given. Keira stood watching enviously. She felt even more left out when Lucy and Harriet went off chatting happily and leaving Keira standing on her own in the changing rooms.

They were all thronging into the school hall. Music was playing and a glitter ball gave a disco effect to the room, spoiled only by several teachers on sentry duty around the room and the tables piled up with food along one side.

A few girls had started to dance but most of the boys were standing in a huddle in the far corner, eyeing the food surreptitiously and pushing each other playfully as they tried to persuade each other to dance.

"Why don't you ask Harriet to dance?"

"You ask her, I'm waiting for something to eat."

"I'd rather dance with Chloe. She's cute."

"Cute? Are you joking? I'd rather dance with Keira than Chloe Richards."

Keira happened to overhear the careless comment and she guessed it wasn't a compliment. Well, she didn't care. Why would she want to dance with any of the boys in the class? They were all horrible. She wished she hadn't come to this party and she wished Lucy hadn't gone off with Harriet because she had no one to talk to now.

She turned with a frown as someone tugged on her sleeve. Could things get any worse? Colin Hopkins was standing beside her and he was wearing the worst shirt she had ever seen. Surely it wasn't purple! And hadn't he brushed his hair today?

"Hi," he said. "I saw you dance in the show, my sister goes to the dance school. I thought you were great."

"Thanks."

What did Colin know about ballet anyway? If anyone saw her talking to swotty Colin that would be the end as far as she was concerned. She wished he would just go away.

"You have a really fresh technique, very simple yet graceful. Although your sautés lacked spring and your glissades weren't slidy enough."

Sautés? *Glissades*? Was this really Colin Hopkins criticizing her ballet moves? She stared at him in surprise.

Colin laughed. "I've watched my sister practise for years. It's all they talk about in my house. Ballet, ballet, ballet. But seriously, I thought you were really good."

"Thanks." This time she meant it. It wasn't just Colin making fun of her. He actually knew what he was talking about.

"Do you want to dance now?"

Dance? With Colin Hopkins? She would never live it down.

He seemed to guess what she was thinking and his face fell. Keira felt sorry for him. He wasn't that bad really. Just because he wasn't good looking like Adam Johnson didn't mean he wasn't kind and clever and funny.

"Oh ok," she said. Hoping that no one would see them if they danced in the corner where they were now. But, before she had time to say anything else Colin had grabbed her by the arm and dragged her right into the middle of the dance floor.

Keira noticed one or two sniggers as Colin bumped into people or stepped on her toes or waved his arms so

64

enthusiastically he nearly smacked her in the face. To her dismay she noticed Adam Johnson was watching them from the huddle of boys in the corner and she wished she could suddenly disappear in a poof of smoke like a real life *Silver Fairy*. She had never felt so relieved as when the music came to an end and she was able to make for the corner of the room to hide in.

"Hey!" A voice called and she felt herself blushing as Adam Johnson stepped in front of her. Oh no, he had seen her dance with Colin.

"You're a really good dancer," Adam told her, his voice reflecting his surprise. "Do you want to dance with me?"

From the corner of her eye she caught sight of Colin and noted his disappointed expression. He had asked her to dance because he thought she was a good dancer. Adam had only asked her to dance with him after he realised that she could actually dance. It was as if he considered her good enough to dance with him. What a big-head.

"No thanks," she said. "I'm dancing with Colin." And she had to try hard not to laugh at the expression on his face.

After that the party didn't seem all that bad. She sat next to Colin at the table and they talked about ballet. She was amazed about how much he knew and the ballets he had actually seen at the theatre. She was actually quite envious and wished she could go to the theatre sometime to see real dancers like Darcey Bussell and Carlos Acosta. He was so lucky.

"I could ask my mum if you can come next time," Colin said. "She won't mind. Debra brings her friends sometimes."

"Oh I couldn't," Keira said, remembering what had happened yesterday. "My mum doesn't really like ballet." And she started to tell Colin all about what had happened after the show. He was a surprisingly good listener and quite mature for his years.

"That's such a shame. And you're a really good dancer. Perhaps your mum doesn't realise how good you are. Does she know anything about it?"

"I guess not. She just thinks it's all showing off."

"There must be a way of explaining to her. We will have to think of a plan."

"No!" Keira protested, remembering what happened after Miss Shelley thought of a plan. "Please don't. It's just a waste of time."

The party had lost some of its gloss now. Colin, sensing that he was the cause tried his best to cheer her up but Keira was just glad when it was time to go home.

Well, that was it. Party over and now two weeks ahead of being stuck in the house with her mother and they still weren't on speaking terms. It wasn't a very appealing prospect.

It was probably the worst Christmas of Keira's life. To make matters worse, twice she had been round to call for Lucy and each time she had been out with Harriet so Keira felt that even her best friend had deserted her.

Christmas day seemed never-ending. The presents she received from her mother, grandmother and two aunties were exactly what she expected to receive. Basically the same as she received every year; socks, pants and vests. The best thing was a book voucher. For a moment she brightened, she could buy another ballet book. Then she remembered what had happened before Christmas and knew that it would be a waste of time. She wasn't going to be having dancing lessons any more.

Perhaps she would buy something from Shakespeare. They had been studying "Romeo and Juliet" at school and she had really enjoyed it. At least it would be something to read for the rest of the holiday. And it would give her a reason to get out of the house for a while. She could go into town and visit the bookshop.

To her dismay, when she mentioned it, her mother decided to come with her. She had been hoping for the chance to get out on her own but her mother had a voucher she wanted to spend as well as a few things she needed from the supermarket. Keira couldn't imagine what; the house was still bursting with Christmas food.

The drive into town was silent and miserable. The voice on the radio was jolly and the music was seasonal but Keira found it annoying.

There was something dismal about shops after Christmas, the decorations looked tatty and the seasonal gifts, now reduced, had an abandoned air about them. Keira knew exactly how they felt. She too had been abandoned, rejected and left in the supermarket.

Just when she thought things couldn't get any worse, who should come round the corner of the High Street but Colin Hopkins. He was with an older, surprisingly pretty girl, and Keira guessed that must be his sister.

"Hi, Keira!" He had called, before she had chance to disguise herself as a normal, happy post-Christmas shopper. "Did you have a nice Christmas?"

She tried to smile, wished she could vanish like the snow that had melted in the sunshine and managed a muttered reply.

"Hey Debs," Colin said to his sister. "This is the girl I was telling you about. She's the one that danced the *Silver Fairy* in your show. I told you she was really good."

67

"Yes, I remember," Debra replied. She turned to Keira and smiled brightly. "You were excellent," she said.

"Thank you," Keira muttered.

She realised her mother was listening and she hoped Colin and Debra wouldn't say anything else. It would just make matters worse. Plus it was rubbing it in that she wasn't allowed to dance anymore.

"Where are you off to?" Colin asked.

"Waterstones," Keira said. "I got a book token for Christmas."

"Me too," Colin told her. "We'll come with you."

Keira looked at her mum enquiringly.

"Yes, that's fine." Her mother agreed. "I will meet you there in an hour. We can go in Woolies for a cup of tea after. Perhaps your friends would like to come too."

To Keira's surprise her mother was smiling encouragingly at Colin and Debra. Even worse, Colin and Debra were smiling back and agreeing to meet her there too.

Oh no. Why did she have to choose today to come into town? And why, of all people, did she have to bump into Colin Hopkins? She couldn't have imagined that happening in her worst nightmare ever.

At least, once they were inside Waterstones, Keira didn't have to worry about her mother listening in. She hastily checked around the store but couldn't see anyone else she knew, which was a relief. Although she quite liked Colin now it wouldn't do to be seen with him out of school.

"I expect you want a book about ballet," Colin said.

"Well no, actually I've got lots of them already. I was thinking of some Shakespeare as we were reading "Romeo and Juliet" last term. I really liked it."

"Me too," Colin agreed. "I've already got a complete set of Shakespeare at home. I prefer the histories myself. I'm just reading "Henry V" at the moment."

Keira was quite surprised. She knew Colin had a reputation as a swot but he was really quite intelligent and very modest with it. The more she got to know him the more she was finding she liked him and it didn't seem to matter that he was podgy and wore glasses. She could talk to him quite easily about almost anything. His sister was really nice too and not the least bit big-headed about her dancing, even though she had been in the local paper and won an important dance trophy.

Keira found herself forgetting all about the disappointment of Christmas. She even told Colin about Lucy and Harriet, although not in a spiteful sort of way, in the way that you would tell a best friend everything that had happened to you since you last met.

Colin found a book he wanted very quickly. To Keira it looked extremely boring, an adult book and not the sort of thing she would read. Debra found several books she liked and couldn't make her mind up and Keira decided to stick to the Shakespeare, despite the fact there were several new stories she would quite like to read. She thought they might look childish and, for some reason, it mattered what Colin and Debra thought of her.

The hour sped by and Keira was surprised when she looked up and saw her mother approaching. Her heart sank slightly and she hoped that no one would mention ballet again now that her mother was back.

"Hello," Mrs Lewis called brightly. "Have you found a book?"

"Yes, mum," Keira said through clenched teeth. How she wished Colin and Debra hadn't agreed to come with them for a cup of tea.

Woolworths was busy. Keira hoped they wouldn't find a table but Debra noticed one where a family were just about to leave.

"Keira, go and sit over there and I'll get you a drink. Orange juice? Did you want some crisps?"

Keira hated it when her mother did that, made her sit at an empty table while she brought the drinks over. She would have liked a coke but knew her mother wouldn't let her but both Debra and Colin were buying coke and crisps. It made her feel childish sitting there with her orange juice in a glass while they drank coke from the can.

Her mother was talking to Debra as if she were an adult, they were talking about clothes and make-up and Debra seemed really interested in Lauren's salon. Lauren told her to pop in sometime and have a facial. Debra said she would. It all seemed very sociable and Keira found it hard to see this person in front of her as her mother, she was a totally different person.

Keira was left to talk to Colin and she managed to steer the conversation away from dance for the rest of the morning. They talked about homework and school and Colin even had the audacity to suggest she might like to come round and borrow some more of his books.

"Oh, I don't think I will have time," Keira said hastily, before her mother had chance to chip in and agree to the idea. Staying at home was bad enough but she didn't fancy spending an afternoon with Colin and Debra.

It was a relief to say good-bye at the end of the road and make their way back to the car park.

"Your friends seem nice, Keira."

"Yes." Keira was non-committal. She didn't want to get into a discussion with her mother just at the moment so she pretended she was engrossed in her book and didn't say anything until they were back at the house.

"Better go and do my homework," Keira muttered and hurried upstairs before her mother had chance to say anything.

In her room she was able to relax. She settled down on her bed with the book and was able to stay there until tea time without being disturbed.

It was the first time ever she was actually looking forward to going back to school.

Chapter ten

When Monday arrived Keira was in two minds whether to call for Lucy or not. She hadn't seen her since the show as she had spent all her time with Harriet during the holidays. Keira knew that Lucy couldn't walk to school with Harriet because she lived on the opposite side of town and was taken to school by her mother in a car.

She was just about to walk straight past the house when she changed her mind. She would call for her after all, the two girls had been friends since nursery school and she wasn't going to let Lucy say that it was her fault they had fallen out.

Keira knocked on the door hesitantly and was relieved to see Lucy open it. Both girls looked at each other then Lucy smiled.

"Hi Keira. I'm nearly ready. Have you done your French homework?"

It was just like old times. The two girls chatted on the way to school, mostly about the show and Keira mentioned that she had bumped into Colin and his sister in town. She said she hadn't realised that Debra went to the dance school too.

Lucy didn't seem all that interested in Colin or Debra and had, just at that moment, spotted Harriet waiting in the playground.

"Hey, Harri!"

"Lucy, I was waiting for you. My mum dropped me off early 'cos she's working today."

Before Keira realised what was happening Harriet had slipped in between the two of them and was manoeuvring Lucy towards their classroom. Keira was left trailing behind the two of them like a lost puppy and she went to sit in her usual place only to find Harriet was sitting there already.

"Oh Keira," Lucy said, looking slightly guilty. "Here, sit here, behind us."

Keira sat down at the desk behind before she had time to think about it and suddenly realised she was being deliberately left out. Lucy had walked to school with her because there was no one else but now she was in school she wanted to be friends with Harriet again. A strange pain stabbed at her heart and, for a moment, she felt tears prick the back of her eyes.

She heard someone sitting in the seat next to her but didn't look up as she didn't want anyone to see the tears in her eyes.

"Hi Keira, can I sit here?"

She recognised the voice. It was Colin. Oh no, that was the last thing she wanted. He would laugh at her and everyone would make fun of her for sitting next to Colin Hopkins. Keira wished he would go away but didn't want to say anything. She didn't want to hurt his feelings like hers had been hurt by Lucy.

Hastily she brushed the tears from her face with the back of her hand and rustled around in her bag pretending to look for her books, even though she knew exactly where they were.

Colin had noticed the tears in her eyes, he also noted that Lucy was sitting next to Harriet now, but he pretended everything was normal as he checked

73

through his French homework, which he knew was perfect anyway.

Miss Lamont walked into the classroom, smiley and bright as usual, and the lesson began. Keira usually enjoyed French and she soon found that she was concentrating on the exercises they had been set.

Colin was also very good at French; in fact he was good at most subjects except sports, and Keira found that she could get on well with him as her partner. Maybe the day wouldn't be so bad after all.

They were on the receiving end of some strange looks as they hung around together but Keira didn't care. Colin was intelligent, sensible and actually quite funny at times. He even offered to walk home with her, which would save the awkwardness of wondering if Lucy was going to wait for her.

Lucy was hanging around by the school gates. She had walked out with Harriet but Mrs Wilson had picked her up and she had driven off, waving cheerfully at Lucy. That meant she either had to walk home on her own or see if Keira would walk with her after being ignored all day.

To Lucy's surprise, Keira walked out with Colin and smiled as she walked past Lucy. But seeing the glum look on her face she felt sorry for her.

"Coming Lucy?" She called. And they all three set off together along the High Street and towards the park. Keira had no idea where Colin lived but he set off quite happily when they came to the library and said he would see them tomorrow.

"Did you sit next to him?" Lucy asked.

"Yes." Keira didn't bother to point out that Lucy had sat next to Harriet all day; it didn't seem to matter now.

As they got to Lucy's house they were just about to say good-bye when Lucy called after her.

"Are you still coming dancing on Saturday?"

"I'm not allowed."

"Well, don't tell your mum then."

"She knows now, she won't let me go any more."

"Oh! See you tomorrow then."

"'Bye Lucy."

Keira somehow had the feeling that things would never be the same again. Everything had changed since Christmas and she knew she had grown up somehow. Life wasn't going to be just how she wanted it to be, she knew that was too much to expect, but now she knew she could deal with most things; disappointment, betrayal and broken dreams. Surely nothing could get any worse.

Her mum was home. Monday was her day off from the salon and she was in the kitchen making tea when Keira got in.

"How was school?" She called from the kitchen.

"The same."

With a sinking feeling Keira realised that life would be the same from now on; school, tea, homework and no dancing. It was all too much for her after the day she had just had and she burst into tears. She was hoping to rush upstairs so no one would hear her but her mother came out of the kitchen just at that moment.

"Keira love, what's wrong?"

It was impossible to try and explain it all. She just shook her head in dismay and confusion.

"Nothing. I don't know." And she managed to escape to her room before her mother could ask her any further questions. Throwing herself on her bed she continued to sob. Why was life so unfair?

There was a tap on the door and her mother stuck her head round.

"Are you alright?"

"Yes, mum," Keira mumbled through her tears.

"You don't look it. Come on love, wash your face and come and have some tea."

Her mum patted her hand kindly. Despite the fact she disapproved of Keira dancing she loved her daughter dearly and couldn't bear to see her so upset. She handed Keira a tissue from the box on the bedside locker.

Keira sat up and blew her nose. She didn't really want any tea but her mum was being nice to her so she would try. Her uniform felt all rumpled. She would need to change first.

"I'll be down in a minute," she said, through a blocked up nose.

Slowly she changed into a pair of jeans and well-loved t-shirt, hung her uniform on the back of the chair and went into the bathroom to wash her face and tidy her hair.

Tea was her favourite, macaroni cheese, but she just couldn't eat it. A few forkfuls were all she could manage and she felt like she was about to choke. She couldn't even eat the strawberry yogurt after and only managed to sip her juice because her throat felt so dry.

After tea she washed up in silence then went straight to her room to do her homework, no arguments about watching TV first. She had some maths to do and it wasn't her favourite subject. Her mind just didn't want to concentrate on fractions and decimals. In the end she gave up and lay on the bed, staring at the ceiling, her mind a whirl of dark shapes and patterns that made no sense at all.

She was still lying there at nine o'clock when she tapped on the door to ask if she wanted any cocoa and biscuits. Usually Keira had her pyjamas on by now and loved to snuggle up on the sofa for half an hour with her mother before she went to bed.

Seeing her laying there her mother was now seriously worried. She went and sat beside her.

"Come on love, tell me what's wrong."

"It's nothing," Keira began. "It's everything. Everything's wrong. Lucy's not my friend any more; she wants to hang out with Harriet. And I miss my dance class, I really enjoyed it. There's just nothing to do now."

"I see. I'm sure you'll find another friend. And what about the Guides? You might enjoy that. Or go swimming, I might even come with you."

"You don't understand. Lucy has been my friend for years. And I love dancing, it's special. When I was the *Silver Fairy* it was like being a real fairy. I was floating, flying, it was magic. I don't want to go to Guides, I want to dance."

"There's no need to make a fuss. Get ready for bed now or you'll be tired at school tomorrow. Don't you think this dancing business is a bit childish?"

"Of course not! Grown-ups are dancers. What about Anna Pavlova, Margot Fonteyn, Darcey Bussell? Colin's sister is sixteen and she still goes to dance classes. I just want to dance."

Lauren sighed heavily. Why did this have to happen? Now of all times? She had enough worries with the salon to run and January was always a bad month for business. Keira had always been a sensible child, until now. And what was she to do about it? Although she had to admit, Keira had danced well in the show, especially considering how few proper lessons she had had.

"Come and have your supper," Lauren said. "It's nearly time for bed."

Once Keira was in bed Lauren sat down with her final cup of coffee and tried to work out what to do. Money was tight but it wasn't just that. The reasons Lauren disliked dance so much went back years and involved many things she didn't want to think about. Things she hadn't thought about since Keira was a baby.

Both of them spent a restless night. Both woke the next day with heavy heads and heavy hearts. Breakfast was a silent affair; neither had much appetite anyway and went their separate ways with gloomy thoughts.

Keira called for Lucy and they walked to school together. Then Lucy drifted off with Harriet and Keira spent the day with Colin. They even sat together at lunch time, munching their sandwiches in glum silence. Unbeknown to Keira, just as the bell was ringing for the end of lunch, a bell was ringing in the dance school and answered in a perfunctory manner by Mrs Dark, the secretary. She took down the message and duly passed it on to Miss Shelley who smiled when she read it. She decided to write a letter in reply and hurried to the office where she sat down at the computer and typed up her suggestions to Mrs Lewis.

The Dance School
21 The High Street

Dear Mrs Lewis,

I would be delighted to have Keira attend my dance classes as previously. She has shown herself to be a dedicated and talented pupil and I am willing to offer similar terms as before. The classes will be offered at a reduced rate providing Keira continues to assist with the younger children.

I hope this will be acceptable to you and look forward to your reply.

Best wishes

Cathy Shelley.

Chapter eleven

Keira could hardly believe it. If it wasn't for the letter in front of her she would have thought she was dreaming it. She could go back to dance lessons. Her mother had agreed with Miss Shelley and she was to return on Saturday. That would mean she had only missed one lesson since the show.

She couldn't wait to tell Lucy. Then she remembered, Lucy wasn't her best friend any more. Never mind, she would still tell her and if Lucy wasn't pleased about the news it wouldn't matter. All that mattered was she would be dancing again.

Even if she hadn't intended to tell Lucy she wouldn't have been able to keep the news back, she was just too excited. The words bubbled out of her as soon as Lucy opened the door.

"Well, that's good news," Lucy agreed. "I wonder why your mum changed her mind."

"Miss Shelley wrote her a letter."

"Really?"

Lucy couldn't help feeling a stab of jealousy. After all, Keira had only been dancing a few months and she had already danced the *Silver Fairy* in the show and now Miss Shelley was writing letters about her. But then, why should she mind? Keira had been her friend for as long as she could remember and she wasn't always showing off like Harriet was. Telling her about the house they lived in, the cars her parents drove – they had one each – the pony she rode at the weekend. Secretly Lucy was starting to feel rather fed up with Harriet.

Suddenly she linked arms with Keira.

"Come on," she said. "Let's sit together in science."

"Ok," Keira agreed.

Neither of the girls liked science all that much and they chose a table at the back of the room. Colin joined them, not bothered in the slightest that the two girls were sitting together, but Harriet looked less than pleased when she came in and found Lucy and Keira together. Reluctantly she sat next to Colin and sulked all through the lesson, refusing to take turns in the experiment they were trying to conduct. Colin was quite happily mixing chemicals and writing furiously as they changed colours, hissed and spat like a witch's spell. He was able to explain exactly what was happening to all three girls and their group got an A at the end of the lesson. The first that Keira and Lucy had ever had in science.

They were well pleased with the result and Lucy shared her crisps with Colin at break time. She had decided he wasn't so bad after all and, as he was such a brain box, it would be a good idea to hang around with him from now on, especially in maths and science lessons.

Saturday was a golden day. Keira packed the ballet shoes and leotard into her backpack; she didn't have to sneak them out this time, and went to call for Lucy. Their class was at nine, then she had to help with the tinies for an hour and the Primary Grade class at eleven. She had remembered to bring a bottle of water with her as Miss Shelley said it was important to drink plenty when you were dancing. She had also brought some fruit to eat after the class. Now that she was dancing seriously she had to start thinking of important things like her diet. She had even agreed to go swimming with her mum once a week, partly as a good way of keeping fit and partly to please her mum. After all, she had agreed to Keira having dance lessons again.

Suddenly the world was full of rainbows. The tinies were sweet and tried to copy everything Keira did. Lucy was her friend again and Colin was quite happy to help them with anything they were stuck with at school. Even the weather was brighter and Keira didn't mind the cold mornings that caught her breath in little swirls as long as the sun shone. Which it did.

Lauren was happier too. It was good to see Keira smiling again. Doing her homework without being told, getting As on her school report and helping in the house without arguing. She was a completely different child these days.

Keira realised it was best not to say too much to her mother about dancing. She spent most of her evenings in her room anyway, homework was soon out of the way and she could read all her ballet books again. Her shelves were full of them as well as the ones she borrowed from the library on a Saturday afternoon.

On Sunday morning she went swimming with her mum and they both found they were enjoying it. Lauren was really pleased to find she had lost weight too and both of them now had an interest in eating healthily. As the weather improved they would be able to manage the occasional trip out, just like they had done when Keira was younger.

Keira's lessons increased from one to two a week. She now went on a Tuesday evening with Lucy and some of the older girls. This was a much more serious class as they would be taking exams in the summer and Keira tried her best to bend and point and stretch just like they did. It was hard work and her legs would ache at the end of the lesson but she knew it was worth it. Every week she could she was a little bit better. Her jétès were higher, her échappés sharper, her arabesques that bit more in line than they had been.

Sometimes Miss Shelley would say, "Well done Keira." And then her heart would sing.

There were days, however, when things didn't go quite so well. She would wobble on her turns, her porte de bras felt like wood and her toes just wouldn't turn out, no matter how hard she tried. On those days she would hurry home and practice in her room until her mother called upstairs for her to stop, she couldn't hear herself think and Corrie was on in a minute so would she mind keeping it down.

"I thought there was a herd of elephants loose," she said light-heartedly. "I was just about to phone the zoo."

But Keira frowned, it was no joking matter. She had to practice until she got it right no matter how long it took.

Now that she was friends with Lucy again the two girls could talk about dance all through their breaks. Harriet soon grew bored; she wanted to talk about her pony all the time and the rosettes she had won at the weekend. Colin was quite happy to listen to their conversations; he even joined in from time to time. His sister was now going to a dance school in Manchester and she wrote home every week so Colin could pass on snippits to the two girls. They found it fascinating. Like pressing their nose to the sweet shop window and dreaming of all the sugar plums inside.

When she wasn't talking, reading or dreaming about ballet she was dancing. Nothing could compare with the feeling of floating on the music, being carried along by crotchets and quavers and swirling like a leaf in the breeze, a feather. Lighter than a gossamer thread on a summer's day. Keira was never happier than when she was dancing. And now she could dance every day.

The weather was improving and it would soon be Easter. There was a gentle warmth in the air, the trees were covering their branches with the new growth of green and golden daffodils were showing their cheery faces.

Mrs Lewis had been to the local garden centre and cheered the front garden up with clutches of pansies and colourful primulas. She hung baskets on either side of the front door and trimmed the forsythia that was rambling over the front wall. Business at the salon was picking up and she was feeling a lot happier now that Keira seemed more settled.

For some reason the sun made her start to think about holidays. It had been years since she and Keira had had a holiday. It would be nice to have a week away somewhere. She thought about Devon where she had spent happy holidays with her grandparents and worked out, if she scrimped and saved a bit, she might be able to afford a week away for her and Keira. That would be nice.

She decided not to say anything in case she couldn't quite manage it and she didn't want Keira to face yet another disappointment. Yes, it would be good for both of them to have a break, especially as Keira would be changing schools in September and it might be the last chance to do something like this.

Mrs Lewis kept a few travel brochures at the salon and poured over them in her breaks. There were a couple of places she really liked the look of and Holly, the Saturday girl, was quite excited about the idea too.

"It would be lovely to have a holiday," Holly said. "I'm saving up to buy a car for when I go to college so I won't be able to have a holiday this year. My boyfriend would like to go abroad but I want to get married when I finish college and Danny says renting is just throwing money away so we need to save up for a deposit. He works in the phone shop on the High Street and he's got a new Peugeot 206."

She chatted on for quite a while unaware that no one was actually listening to her as Lauren had returned to her brochure and the customer having her high-lights done had practically dozed off.

Keira had no idea what her mother was planning. She had been visiting her new school with the rest of her class and had one or two worries about the whole thing. They would finish later for a start and there seemed to be a lot of talk about homework. She wondered how she would manage it all with her dance classes and Miss Shelley had even mentioned the possibility of her learning tap as well.

She discussed it with Lucy who didn't seem to think it was a problem, but then she didn't have to help with the tinies and Grade Ones as payment for her lessons. How was she going to fit it all in?

Keira mentioned this one Saturday morning to Miss Shelley when they were having a break between classes.

"You really are taking your dancing very seriously, aren't you?"

"Oh yes, it's the most important thing in my life. I don't mind if I don't do so well at my new school as long as I can have my dance lessons."

"Now Keira, you must work really hard at your school lessons too. They are equally important. Do you realise that most people who have dancing lessons don't become actual dancers when they grow up so it's important to have your GCSEs too."

"I know that. I just mean I want to do really well in my dancing, more than I want to in French or Maths for example. And even if I don't become an actual ballerina I could be a teacher or something."

This made Miss Shelley smile. Sometimes she thought that teaching children to dance was just as hard as dancing in a company, as she had in her younger years. Not that she didn't enjoy it of course. And when you found a child that showed promise, as Keira did, that made it all worthwhile. It didn't matter how many hours she worked, watching a child with determination and talent improve bit by bit was a joy indeed.

But she could understand Keira's worries, after all, she had struggled herself when she first went to secondary school and all she had wanted to do was dance. Then it came to her. Stageschool! If Keira went to Stageschool as she herself had then she wouldn't have to worry about homework and dance lessons after school, it was all part of the day.

"There are always Stageschool and Dance Academies," she said. "Have you ever thought about that? You would have all your dance lessons in the morning and school lessons in the afternoon. There are several in this area. Quite a few pupils from here have gone on to Stage schools."

"I know, Colin's sister goes to one in Manchester."

"Yes, Debra Hopkins. She was one of our exceptional students. Would you like to do something like that?"

Keira's heart pounded with excitement. Would she like it? Of course she would. But like a pin in a birthday balloon she knew it wasn't possible. She could only have these lessons because she helped with the tinies; there was no way her mum could pay for her to go to a Stageschool. Lessons, uniform, everything, and she would have to stay there during the week like Debra did.

Just as quickly as her spirits rose they sank again, this time to the tips of her toes and her face fell too.

"My mum wouldn't let me, there's no way she could afford to send me to Stageschool."

"There are things called scholarships, bursaries, grants even for promising students. I'm sure you get could some help with the fees, possibly even the uniform."

This time Keira didn't allow her hopes to rise too high. Even if they could afford it her mum had been very reluctant to allow her to dance at all. Much less would she allow her to go away to a boarding school where she would only be back at the weekends. It was an impossible dream.

"I still don't think she would like it."

"Look, don't say anything just yet. I will find out some information for you. We usually get prospectus sent to us at this time of the year ready for pupils starting in September. There are a couple in the office now. I will bring them with me next lesson and you can take them home to show your mum."

"Ok."

Keira was less than convinced that her mum would be anyway near open to the suggestion of her going to dance school but she could always dream. And if there was even the remotest of possibilities then Keira would do everything she could to go to Stageschool.

Chapter twelve

Miss Shelley was as good as her word and brought the prospectuses to the Tuesday evening class. Several of the girls were interested in them and she had to share them out, telling them to show their parents and bring them back next week.

Keira knew there would be no point showing her mother. Not even with the chance of scholarships and bursaries would her mother consider the possibility of Keira going to Stageschool. But the more she thought about it the more she loved the idea. Imagine, a school where she could learn to dance as well as continuing with ordinary lessons. And having classes with other students who understood all about wanting to dance, how important it was to your life, not just a hobby or something you did on a Saturday morning but something you did every day for the rest of your life.

To Keira that was an amazing thought. She had hidden the brochure under her pillow and read it every night. She knew it off by heart, the names of the teachers, the different types of dance they studied, the dancers who had gone on to successful careers on the stage. There were pictures of the lucky girls, and a couple of boys, on stage in different roles, wearing lovely costumes, dancing in all kinds of interesting places.

And Keira would fall asleep dreaming that the next student to have her picture in the brochure would be her, Keira Lewis, or should she change her name to something more exotic? She tried to imagine herself as Anna or Alicia or Marguerite but it didn't seem like her somehow. Keira drifted off to the sound of applause and bouquets thrown onto the stage from an adoring audience.

Mrs Lewis had received a letter. It was about the new school Keira was due to start in September. She opened it at the breakfast table on Saturday morning and groaned at the length of the uniform list.

"Do you really need all this stuff?" She asked out loud.

"It's not my fault," Keira muttered, wondering what her mother would say to a list that included ballet shoes, tap shoes, jazz shoes, leotards, tutus, headbands and hairslides. She knew there was just no chance of it ever happening and she tried to push the thought to the back of her mind. At least she was having dance lessons now, something she wouldn't have thought possible a few months ago. That was something to be grateful for, she guessed. But it was hard to feel grateful when all she wanted to do was dance, day and night, night and day, just dance, dance, dance, dance, dance.

On Tuesday evening the talk was all about the Stageschool. Cherry Thornton was all excitement because her parents had said she could go for the audition in the summer holidays. If she was successful she would get a place at the school. The other girls were completely envious when Cherry told them all about it.

Keira could hardly speak she was so jealous. Why oh why didn't she have the sort of parents who wanted you to do well, who were proud of you when you said you wanted to be a dancer? Why did her mother get angry every time she even mentioned the subject and was reluctant to have anything to do with the most important thing in Keira's life?

Of course Cherry had to tell Miss Shelley who said she was really pleased for her and offered to give her extra lessons to help her prepare for the audition.

Keira felt like crying. Her heart just wasn't in the dancing tonight, her toes weren't pointy enough, her arms weren't graceful enough, her jumps weren't springy enough and her arabesques wobbled. She hoped Miss Shelley hadn't noticed, the teacher hadn't said anything so perhaps she was so busy concentrating on Cherry that she wasn't really thinking about the rest of the class.

It was almost a relief when the lesson was over and Keira was hoping she could sneak out of the room un-noticed when Miss Shelley's voice stopped her in her tracks.

"Keira! Have you a moment please?"

"Yes Miss Shelley."

"Is anything wrong? You seemed to be struggling a bit today."

"I'm sorry Miss Shelley. It's just all that about the Stageschool and Cherry is going to go and I would love to have an audition but I know it would be absolutely hopeless asking my mum about it, she even complained about hockey boots for my new school..." And Keira burst into tears, much to her embarrassment.

Miss Shelley handed her a tissue from the box on top of the piano.

"For a start, just because Cherry has an audition doesn't mean she will get a place at the school. There are hundreds of children apply every year and only a dozen or so get a place. Secondly, she is nearly fourteen and that's a good age to be going away to school, too young can cause all sorts of problems. And thirdly, you must never give up. If dancing is what you really want to do there will be a way. I can't tell you what it is right now, I know you have all kinds of problems at home, but nothing is impossible if you have determination. You are a very talented dancer but you are young yet, sometimes it's not a good thing to experience too much pressure too soon. It can actually spoil your dancing instead of improving it."

Keira hiccupped back a sob. She knew Miss Shelley was trying to be kind but she didn't understand, all Keira wanted to do was dance. Nothing else mattered. And somehow she would find a way, with or without Miss Shelley's help.

"Run along now, you don't want to be late home. I will see you on Saturday. It's good to have dreams but just enjoy dancing for now."

"Yes Miss Shelley."

But something had stirred in Keira's heart. Whatever it took she would go to Stageschool. She knew that was what she wanted and what she needed to become a real dancer, like the girls in the brochure, she would be a dancer. Her mind was made up.

Keira studied the prospectus with extra concentration. There was a form in the back of the book to fill in to apply for an audition. It had to be signed by a dance teacher and a parent. Surely Miss Shelley wouldn't object to signing it but how would she get her mother to agree?

She pondered it over and over during the next few days. Could she get her mother to sign it without realising what it was? Pretend it was for a school trip or something? Could she get someone else to sign it?

Lucy's mum for instance. Could she ask Lucy to pretend it was hers?

None of the options seemed very honest. It bothered Keira that she might have to lie to people, especially her mother, and what would happen when they found out? She wouldn't be allowed to go to the school then so it would all have been for nothing. Was there no way round it? There must be something she could do. She wasn't the sort of girl to just give up.

Keira decided to mention it to Lucy and Colin at lunch break the next day. Now that the weather was getting warmer they were allowed on the field at lunch time so they found a quiet corner, put their coats on the grass and sat down.

Keira pulled the brochure out of her school bag.

"What's that?" Colin asked.

Keira showed him. "It's the Stageschool I want to go to but I don't think my mum would sign the form for the audition."

"Oh, that's a shame. You are really good, even Debra thinks so and she goes to dance school already."

"Lucky her."

"Perhaps she could help you."

"What do you mean?"

"I don't know but I will ask her if she has any ideas when I see her at the weekend."

"Hmm." Keira was doubtful but she thought it was nice of Colin to suggest it.

"Yes, there must be something you can do," Lucy put in, not wanting to be left out. She didn't want the other two to think she was jealous or anything. It hadn't bothered her that Cherry Thornton had got an audition but she didn't see why Keira shouldn't have a go too. Perhaps she could ask her mum if she could go for an audition. She had been dancing longer than Keira and

91

she was just as good. Yes, she would ask her mum tonight. But that would seem unfair to Keira. She would have to do something to help her friend or they would all think she was being selfish.

The three put their heads together, determined to come up with a plan.

How could they persuade Keira's mother to let her audition for the Stageschool? They all agreed that she was good enough to get a place, even Debra had said so and she should know, she went to a famous dance school already and she was going to be a cygnet in Swan Lake.

Everyone was so envious of her. Especially Keira, who fell asleep at night to the music of *Lac des Cygnets* and saw herself floating in a feathery tutu under a single spotlight on an empty stage. She twirled and twirled and twirled until she disappeared into a silver mist surrounding a frozen lake.

Chapter thirteen

It was Lucy that came up with the solution. "Of course!" She exclaimed. "It's obvious."
Keira and Colin looked at her enquiringly, they were in the middle of their lunch and they received a few odd looks, Lucy waving a sandwich in her hand and Keira just about to take a bite out of her apple.
"What is?" Colin asked, putting his bag of crisps down on the table and wondering if Lucy was feeling alright.
"It's simple. The *Silver Fairy*!"
"What?" Colin asked but Keira was starting to follow her friend's train of thoughts. She finished her mouthful of apple.
"You don't mean..?"
"Of course, it's simple. Keira can go to the audition instead of me. My mother has signed the form and so has Miss Shelley. If Keira goes instead of me then everyone will know how good she is and her mum will have to let her go to Stageschool."
"But what will your mum say?" Keira asked Lucy. "Won't she be cross?"
"I expect she will at first but if we explain to her about your mum not letting you go then she will understand."
Keira wasn't so sure; after all, it cost quite a lot to even go to the audition. And how would she get there? The

Stageschool might not know the difference between Keira and Lucy but Mrs Green would.

"We will just ask if you can come with me," Lucy went on. "Then, when I go to get changed, you get changed instead and do the audition."

Colin was totally flabbergasted. Were they serious? He could just imagine how furious both mothers would be when they found out.

"What if I don't get a place?" Keira asked. It would be much worse than when she had danced the *Silver Fairy*, then it had been to help Lucy out, now it seemed rather selfish to take someone's chance of a place at Stageschool, after all, it was everyone's dream who wanted to be a dancer.

"I can't do it," Keira said. "It wouldn't be fair. It's your chance to get a place there."

"But I could try again," Lucy said. "If I explain it was all my idea, that I wanted you to have a chance too. Please Keira. Wouldn't it be great if we both got a place at the Stageschool?"

"Well yes," Keira agreed, but somehow it didn't seem very likely and she knew everyone would be furious. Lucy really was crazy if she thought it was even worth talking about.

"You two would really be for it, big time," Colin said, picking up the discarded crisps and finishing them off, tipping the packet up to collect the crumbs in the bottom.

Keira was turning the idea round and round in her head. Could she? No, of course not, it was ridiculous. But then, she had danced the *Silver Fairy*. No, of course she couldn't. This was probably against the law or something.

"How can it be against the law?" Lucy said. "I said you could take my place."

"But I would be pretending to be you. It's fraud or something."

"I'll ask my dad," Colin said. "He knows about that sort of thing."

"But you will come with me, won't you?" Lucy asked, now that she had the idea in her head she couldn't let it go. "Please Keira."

"Well, I guess that would be ok," Keira agreed, although how she would feel seeing her friend get the thing she had been dreaming of for the last few months, she didn't know.

Colin remained silent, raising his eyebrows as if to say they were both completely mad, then took a banana out of his lunch box and peeled it thoughtfully.

"When is this audition?" he asked.

"Two months time," Lucy said.

"Well, whoever is going to go to the audition you had better get cracking," and he packed his lunch box away, wiping his hands on his trousers before getting up from his seat. "I'm going to computer club, I'll see you later."

"Ok."

Both girls finished their lunch in silence, mulling their thoughts around in their heads. Lucy was wondering if she should have made the suggestion in the first place, would it be too much if Keira got the place and she didn't? How would she feel then? It had seemed a good idea at the time but she would be really devastated if Keira went to Stageschool and she didn't. And what would her mother say? It was alright to act confident in front of the others but secretly she knew her mother would be terribly disappointed.

But she couldn't back down now that she had made the offer. Maybe she half hoped that Keira wouldn't take her up on it anyway, she obviously had her doubts about the whole thing. It depended just how much Keira really wanted to dance.

"Well, I suppose I could come with you," Keira said hesitantly, as they made their way to maths that afternoon. "Just to see what it's like."

Both girls knew that Keira would go to the audition instead of Lucy, both kept their fingers crossed that they wouldn't get found out until it was too late and both of them hoped that Keira would get a place at Stageschool.

The Tuesday evening classes were becoming more intense as the girls practised the routines they would need for their auditions. Not only were Lucy and Cherry going for an audition at the Stageschool but another girl, Alice Sims, had an audition for the Royal Ballet School and Miss Shelley thought she had a good chance of getting a place. And of course, Keira was working just as hard in case she got the chance to take Lucy's place on the day.

They didn't think anyone suspected anything as several of the girls were learning pieces for auditions in a local production of *Annie* and Becky Jones was hoping for a place in a national talent competition shown on TV.

It was a busy time and tempers were often fraught, especially if one girl thought others were getting more of Miss Shelley's attention than they were. Becky was becoming right stuck up and everyone was getting very tired of her diva behaviour.

"She hasn't even got a place yet," Cherry whispered to Keira. "And I doubt she will, every time she turns that pirouette she wobbles, no matter how many times Miss Shelley has to tell her to 'spot'. Her head still turns way too early."

Keira agreed but she was far too busy perfecting her own routines to worry about Becky's wobbles or anything else for that matter. She had to be perfect. She couldn't let Lucy down. Imagine taking her place and then not getting into the Stageschool. It would be terrible for both of them.

Mrs Green had agreed to Keira coming along with them. It would be the school holidays by then and she couldn't see a problem. She assumed, of course, that Keira's mum had agreed to it and she was in too much of a whirl herself to think that there could be any plot afoot.

The day drew nearer. The girls worked harder. Only a week left of school. Then the bombshell dropped.

"I have been thinking," Mrs Lewis said, as they sat down for tea on Saturday evening. "It's about time we had a holiday."

"Oh?" Keira didn't know why she suddenly had a sinking feeling in the pit of her stomach, as if she were about to jump off a diving board from a very great height.

"Yes. It's a couple of years since we went away anywhere and I thought a week in a caravan would be nice. Somewhere by the sea."

Keira could hear her heart pounding in her ribs. Why had this sudden sense of foreboding come over her?

"You've only got another week left at school and then we could go. It would make a change for us both, something special before you go to your new school."

The audition! That was the first week of the holidays. She couldn't possibly miss that but how could she tell her mother she couldn't go on holiday without telling her why? And what would her mother say if she said she would rather go to an audition with Lucy than on holiday with her mother? Oh, why did this have to happen?

"Keira? What do you think?"

Keira was thinking rapidly. "A holiday would be nice, but I have promised Lucy I will go somewhere with her that week. Couldn't we go another time?"

"You would rather go somewhere with Lucy than go on holiday for a week? What's so important that Lucy needs you to go with her? And no, I can't have another week off. I couldn't afford to close down the salon and that's the only week I can get cover."

What could she say? Mrs Lewis always thought that people who wanted to dance were shallow, show-off sort of people. If Keira told her she wanted to go to an audition with Lucy her mother just wouldn't understand. She searched her brain for another reason she might want to go somewhere with Lucy but nothing came to her. Besides, she knew she couldn't lie to her mother.

"Lucy's got an audition at the Stageschool. She really wants me to go with her. It's really important."

"Is that all? An audition? And you want to go with her? Don't be so silly."

"Oh please mum, I really want to go."

Mrs Lewis looked at her daughter's pleading face. She always knew these dance lessons were a big mistake. Dancers were all the same, selfish, inconsiderate people who thought of nothing but their dancing. She had seen it all before.

"Well, you're not!" Mrs Lewis shouted. "We are going on holiday. I have already decided. Lucy doesn't need you to go with her. How do you know her mother will let you go anyway?"

"She has already said I can. Oh please, mum."

There were tears in Keira's eyes now.

Mrs Lewis was really annoyed now. Keira and Lucy must have already asked Lucy's mum. They had been working it all out behind her back and she wouldn't even have known about it if she hadn't mentioned the holiday. She couldn't blame the Greens of course; they knew nothing about the holiday. Neither did Keira, come to that. And if it meant so much to her she would only sulk on the holiday and ruin it for both of them.

Mrs Lewis got up crossly and went into the kitchen to wash up. Really! These girls and their ideas. They were so headstrong at that age, not like when she was younger. Then they had just done as they were told and no nonsense.

She sighed as Keira came in with the rest of the plates. Was it worth booking the holiday if Keira was going to be so upset about it all? But she had been looking forward to a week away herself and she had managed to save up just enough for one of those caravans in the brochure.

The thoughts were whirling around in her head as she tried to sleep that night. In the end she decided to give Mrs Green a ring, have a chat with her, find out what exactly was going on with this audition business.

"Hello, it's Lauren Lewis. Keira's mum. I am just ringing about this audition thing next week."

"Oh, hello Lauren. Karen Green. Yes, that's fine. I don't mind Keira coming along at all. Might make Lucy feel less nervous. No, no, it's not a problem. And we won't be too late back. Perfectly fine. Good-bye."

That hadn't been quite what Mrs Lewis had been trying to ask but somehow she hadn't had the chance to say what was on her mind.

Well, she guessed she could keep the money for another holiday. It seemed a shame for them to miss out. But why did she have this strange feeling that something wasn't quite right? That there was something nobody was telling her? What was Keira up to this time?

Chapter fourteen

Keira knew she had to look immaculate for the audition but she only had one leotard and that was not at its best, being an old one of Lucy's. Only her shoes had been new and she had had to save up for those herself.

Lucy had said she could borrow her new leotard for the audition, although it might be slightly too big, but the shoes would have to be her own because it wasn't good to wear someone else's. The ribbons were looking slightly frayed but her ankle socks were as white as they could possibly be as she had slipped them into the washing machine with the towels as Keira knew her mother liked them to be brighter than bright.

She arrived at Lucy's house early as they had arranged to do each other's hair, brushing it up into the smoothest bun ever, pinning it with as many hair grips as they could find and spraying it with a whole can of hairspray Keira had found in her mum's room.

They just hoped that Lucy's mum wouldn't notice that both girls had their hair tide up instead of only Lucy, or, if she did notice that she wouldn't think there was anything strange about it.

Luckily, Mrs Green was too busy fussing over Lucy to even glance at Keira and, if she wondered why Keira had her dance bag, she didn't say anything. She was checking for the hundredth time that Lucy had everything she needed, that they had the letter from the Stageschool and that she knew exactly where she was going as she was driving them there in the car.

The two girls sat in the back of the car. It was hard to tell which was the most nervous out of them and Keira was more worried that someone would guess their secret, though how they could was difficult to know. No one at the Stageschool had seen either of them before.

They had to be there by ten o'clock as Lucy's audition was in the morning and there were several parts to it, including a medical examination and a written test.

There were about ten other girls and their mothers all standing nervously in the foyer of the school when they arrived. A lady with a clipboard was calling out names and handing out badges with numbers on.

"Quick," Lucy whispered to Keira. "Over here."

She pulled her to one side, away from her mother, as she didn't want her to see the lady giving the badge to Keira instead of to Lucy.

"Lucy Green?"

"Yes," Keira answered nervously as Lucy gave her a helpful nudge in the ribs. It was hard to remember to be Lucy instead of herself.

Keira took the badge; with number nine printed on it in red, and fumbled around pretending she couldn't get it to fasten on her.

"Don't worry," the lady said. "Just pin it on your leotard before you come into the studio. Don't forget now."

"I won't," Keira said, keeping her face down so the lady wouldn't get a good look at her. She must see so many girls coming for auditions that it was hardly likely she would remember one in particular. They all looked pretty much the same in leotards and pink shoes with their hair scraped back in buns.

Lucy noticed that her mum was coming over.

"Quick," she said to Keira. "This way." And they hurried into a changing room where there were several other girls already changing.

Luckily, parents weren't allowed in so Lucy knew her mother couldn't follow her in and she wouldn't know it was actually Keira that went in for the audition.

"Number seven," the lady called.

A girl in a pink leotard stood up, pulled her leotard down at the back and rubbed her hands together nervously.

"Good luck," someone else whispered. And the girl smiled thankfully.

A few minutes later the sound of music trickled through from the other room and the familiarity of it helped to quell some of the nerves. It was just like a lesson. One girl started to do pliés in the corner of the room and Keira wanted to join in. Concentrating on the familiar exercises made her feel much better and it was quite a surprise when she heard someone calling out:

"Number nine. Number nine?"

Lucy pushed her. "That's you," she whispered.

"Oh."

Keira looked up quickly and followed the lady out of the room into a large, sunny studio where two more ladies and one man were sat behind a polished desk. They had sheets of paper in front of them and lady smiled kindly at Keira.

"Hello dear. I am Mrs Fox; this is Monsieur Raymond and Miss Stevenson. Now try not to worry, we just want you to do your best. Take your place by the barre and we will start with some elementary exercises."

As the first few notes from the piano tinkled across the room Keira felt herself relax. She had done this so many times. It was as if the music took over and was telling her what to do. Bend, two, three, hold, two three, straight, two, three. Her arm raised and lowered, her head moved automatically as she followed her hand with her eyes. The music told her when to stretch and point and turn. It was like a heart beat pulsing through her and it made her feel more alive, more real than she did when she wasn't dancing.

"Very good, dear. Now we would like to see your set piece. Take your place in the centre of the room."

This was the bit that Keira liked best. Now she could be free to dance how she wanted to dance. The music would prompt her but it was her soul that told her how to dance. She loved every minute of it, her body soaring and floating just like she wanted it to.

The silence as the music finished filled the room and, for a moment, Keira was aware of three pairs of eyes on her and she felt like the entire universe was holding its breath.

"Very nice, dear," Mrs Fox said. "Now you can return to the changing rooms and Mrs Penny will be along in a minute to tell you what to do next."

Keira curtsied just like she had been taught, first to the centre, then to the left, then the right and finally the centre again. Then, on tip-toes she ran from the room and back into the changing room to find number ten in floods of tears with some of the other girls trying to comfort her and a flustered Mrs Penny holding the clip board like a talisman.

"You will be fine, dear," she was telling the sobbing number ten. "Here, take my handkerchief and blow your nose." It was a mystery to her why young girls failed to carry handkerchiefs these days but hers had come into use on many occasions over the years.

"I can't," number ten wailed. "I can't go in; I can't remember any of the steps. I don't know what to do."

"It's alright," Keira told her. "It's really not that bad. It's just like a class really and they're all very nice. Don't cry. You've smudged your make-up. Look, blow your nose and I will do your mascara again for you. You will be fine, I promise you."

The girl looked at her doubtfully and Mrs Penny, seeing a glimmer of hope, took her by the hand and led her to door.

"Remember to curtsey, dear" she whispered. "No one will eat you."

Number ten managed a wan smile at that, sniffed loudly, took a deep breath and disappeared into the room.

"Thank you, dear," Mrs Penny whispered to Keira. "Now come along with me, the doctor would like to ask you a few questions."

Keira could see Lucy's face staring at her anxiously and she managed a quick smile before she followed Mrs Penny over to the medical room where a man in a white coat asked her lots of questions about her back and wanted to see her feet. He measured her and weighed her then made her bend down and touch her toes all the time muttering, "Hm. Fine. Fine. Very good. Excellent."

Keira was starting to feel like a horse and wondered if he would want to see her teeth next to try and work out how old she was.

"Date of birth?" The doctor asked and Keira was just about to give her own when she remembered she was supposed to be Lucy. When was Lucy's birthday? She knew it was in May sometime because she had been to her party but what year was she born? It must be the same as her as they were in the same year at school. At least she hoped so as she gave the date to the doctor.

"You can go back and change now," he told her. "This afternoon there will be a written test."

At last Keira could have the chance to tell Lucy about the audition. She hurried back into the changing rooms and found that number ten was no longer in floods of tears, just coming out of the studio her face was wreathed in smiles and she was following Mrs Penny across to the medical room.

"Thank you," she called when she saw Keira and Keira smiled in return, glad to do something to help.

"Well?" Lucy asked. "How did it go? You better tell me all the details 'cos my mum will want to know."

"It really wasn't that bad," Keira began, as she untied her shoes and folded them neatly. She handed the borrowed leotard back to Lucy and quickly changed back into her outdoor clothes. She described the audition in as much detail as she could but failed to explain the wonderful feeling she had experienced as she had danced in front of the three adjudicators.

As soon as they saw Mrs Green she wanted to know how Lucy had got on.

"How did it go? Did you enjoy yourself? Do you think you did ok?"

Lucy blushed, not wanting to lie to her mother and suddenly feeling caught out.

"It was ok," she muttered. "I'm hungry now. We've to have something to eat and meet back at the reception desk at two o'clock. There's a written exam this afternoon."

"Oh, you'll have no problem with that," Mrs Green said. Lucy was clever enough in school, her grades were always As and she had passed her eleven plus with flying colours.

"Yes mum. Come on Keira, let's find the cafeteria."

The two girls hurried along the corridor, following a group of girls and their mothers; including number ten who was actually called Chloe and was quite pretty now that her dark eyes weren't swimming with tears and her face was no longer red and blotchy.

"Hey, come and sit with us," she called, but Keira didn't want any questions being asked them so they slowed down and pretended they had to sit with Lucy's mum.

The atmosphere in the cafeteria was buzzing; the girls could now relax as the worst part of the audition was over, as far as most of them were concerned. There was only a written exam to do and most of them found that less worrying than the actual dancing. After all, it was the dancing that counted at the Stageschool, surely.

Another group of children were already in the cafeteria. Their auditions were going to start in the afternoon and they had already done the written exam. To her shock, Keira noticed Cherry Thornton. She had forgotten that she had an audition at the Stageschool too. What if she noticed them?

Keira tried to catch Lucy's eye so she could warn her but she was too busy listening to her mum giving advice for the afternoon's exam.

They ate sandwiches and drank juice, Mrs Green had a cup of tea and a scone, Keira and Lucy had some fruit and a shortbread biscuit.

"Hey Keira, Lucy!" It was Cherry, she had seen them.

"How did you get on?" She asked Lucy.

"Ok," Lucy replied, wishing they could leave, or that Cherry would, but she seemed in no hurry to go.

106

"I've got my audition next," she told them. "It must be really terrifying."

"Not really," Keira said. Then remembered it wasn't her who was supposed to have had the audition.

They were relieved to see Mrs Penny re-appearing with the clip board.

"Group one, follow me please. Group two, make your way to the changing rooms and change for your audition."

Lucy took Keira's arm and they hurried out together before they could be asked any more questions.

"You go for the exam," Lucy whispered. "I'll go and wait somewhere so my mum doesn't see me. We'll meet after by the reception."

"Ok."

"And good luck."

"Thanks."

Keira disappeared into the hall where the exam was to take place and Lucy went to find somewhere to wait. It was quite easy to slip away un-noticed and she found herself in a small study with several desks, a bookcase and a blackboard. She spent some moments browsing among the books and finally found something that looked interesting, a biography of several famous dancers, and she sat down at one of the desks to read it.

Lucy began to wonder what it would be like to actually go to the Stageschool and, for the first time, she wondered how she would feel if Keira got the place instead of her.

It was too late now. Keira would be taking the exam. She would either have the place or she wouldn't, there was nothing Lucy could do about it now.

An hour later the exam was over and Lucy and Keira had to appear at the reception desk at exactly the same time to avoid suspicion. Lucy heard the door open and a hub-bub of relieved voices, glad that it was finally over.

"Keira, over here."

The two girls stood side by side, grinning with relief.

Mrs Penny re-appeared with the clip board.

"Well done to all of you," she said. "And thank you all for coming. You will each receive a letter in the post in about two week's time informing you of the decision. Now, I will just take all your badges back. When I call your name please hand it in to me. Mary Phillips. Ellie Smith. Jenny Roper. Lucy Green. Susan..."

"That's not Lucy Green," a voice called out. "That's Keira Lewis!"

All eyes turned to regard her in surprise. Both Lucy and Keira stared at Cherry Thornton in horror and Mrs Penny stood, mouth open, clip board in hand. The whole room was frozen into silence.

Chapter fifteen

Keira and Lucy were sitting outside the principal's office waiting for Mrs Green who was inside with Mrs Fox and Miss Stevenson.

"I knew we shouldn't have done it," Keira said, miserably. "Now my mum will go mad and I'll never be able to dance again, not after last time."

"Now neither of us will get a place at Stageschool," Lucy said, following her own train of thoughts. What had she been thinking of suggesting this crazy idea? If only she hadn't, she might now have been selected instead of sitting in disgrace outside the principal's office.

The door opened and Mrs Green came out looking grim-faced.

"Really, you two girls. Haven't you learnt your lesson by now? You had better go in, Madame will see you now."

They both rose reluctantly and went into the room together. It was a surprisingly large and sunny room, an observation they failed to make under the present circumstances. Instead their eyes were drawn to the figure behind the desk. The elderly lady was gaunt and sat upright in a high-backed chair. She had piercing blue eyes and silver hair drawn tightly away from her face so it almost looked like she had no hair at all. A fur cape was draped around her shoulders and she wore a high-necked, white blouse. She regarded the girls intently, as if she could see straight through them.

"Well?" She demanded icily. "What is the meaning of this?"

Keira felt a warm flush rising in her cheeks. She glanced sideways at Lucy who was hanging her head, staring at her shoes. Neither girl spoke.

A rustle in the corner reminded them that Mrs Fox and Miss Stevenson were still in the room. Even they seemed to have cowed before the striking figure of Madame.

"We're sorry," Keira managed to whisper.

"Sorry?"

"Yes," Lucy echoed. "We're sorry."

"It was my fault," Keira said. "I changed places with Lucy."

"And why exactly?" Madame enquired.

"Because my mum wouldn't let me apply for the Stageschool and I really wanted to. She doesn't like me dancing and it's all I want to do. Just to dance. I thought it might show her that I could do it and then she would agree. We didn't mean to cause any trouble."

"It was my idea," Lucy admitted. "It was all because of the *Silver Fairy* and I thought it would prove that Keira really could dance and then her mum would let her go to Stageschool."

"The *Silver Fairy*?" Madame stared at the girls in a way that brought them both to silence.

"I don't think they meant any harm," Mrs Fox tried to say but she was stopped by a steely look from Madame.

"The thing to decide is what is to be done with you. I understand that Lucy's mother paid for the audition and that Keira's mother knows nothing about it. I have

110

decided that Lucy will have a chance to try for a place, that is only fair. There will be more auditions at Easter and Lucy will have her chance then. Now you will all leave me, you have taken up enough of my time. I will write to both of your parents and inform them of this disgraceful episode and the outcome. Now go!"

Keira burst into tears. She was unable to move even though she wanted nothing more than to get out of the room and as far away from the Stageschool as she possibly could.

Mrs Fox rose from her chair and took both girls by the hand, leading them out of the room.

"There, there," she murmured to them. "Madame's bark is much worse than her bite. Go home now and try and forget all about this. You really have been silly girls but no harm was done. Come on now, dear."

In the corridor Mrs Green was waiting and she put her arms round Lucy.

"Don't cry now. Come on you two, let's get you home. I don't know what you were thinking of. All this bother you've caused and I don't know what your mother will say, Keira."

"I'm really sorry, Mrs Green," Keira sniffed.

Mrs Green handed her a tissue, why was it that no one carried handkerchiefs these days? She took both girls by the arm and led them outside where the sun was still shining and everything seemed normal. As if nothing untoward had ever happened.

Keira could hardly believe what they had done. Before it had all seemed exciting and daring, now it seemed silly and rather immature. And she knew she would be in dreadful trouble when she got home.

The journey back was silent. Neither Keira nor Lucy could think of anything to say to each other and Mrs Green was too annoyed to speak. After all she had done Lucy hadn't even had an audition. The Stageschool had said she had could have another try but Mrs Green wasn't sure she wanted to go through the whole thing again. Surely Lucy couldn't have wanted it that badly or she wouldn't have let Keira take her place. It was all so terribly annoying. In fact, the more she thought about it, the angrier she grew. She would have a few things to say when they got back.

"I will drop you at home," Mrs Green told Keira, as if she were afraid Keira might disappear somewhere in a cloud of smoke.

"'Bye," Keira said, as she slipped out of the car.

She wondered if her mother would be in and what on earth she could say to her. To her relief the house was empty and she was able to sneak upstairs and put her ballet bag away before anyone noticed it. Then she sat on the edge of her bed, her head in her hands, and waited for her mum to come home.

Of course, Mrs Lewis didn't have an inkling that anything was wrong and she was so busy making tea when she got in that she almost forgot to ask Keira how she had got on on her day out with Lucy.

"It was ok," Keira said, then quickly changed the subject. "There's a film on TV I would like to watch tonight, it's about Shakespeare. Can I watch it? It's at 8 o'clock."

"I guess so. Can you give me a hand with the washing up, please?"

Keira knew that the peace wouldn't last forever. The Stageschool had said that they would write to both the parents so she knew a letter would arrive sooner or later, and then her mother would find out everything. She half toyed with the idea of telling her mother anyway but she couldn't think how to bring it up. "By the way mum, when I went with Lucy last weekend we changed places and I did the audition instead of her."

Somehow she couldn't see her mum being very understanding about the whole thing. She just didn't understand how important it was for Keira to dance and, that starting her new school in September would mean she would have very little time for classes. Just when she should be doing more dancing not less. She needed to catch up with the other girls her age, some who had been dancing since they were three, and Miss Shelley had said it would be a good idea for her to learn tap as well. She couldn't see her mother agreeing to that.

The letter arrived on Friday. It had the Stageschool crest on the front and, for a wild moment, Keira thought about throwing it in the recycling, or hiding it somewhere, but she knew her mum would find out eventually and then she would be in even more trouble.

All day she moped around the house waiting for her mum to come home from work, too nervous to do anything she spent most of the time sprawled in front of the television, not the least bit interested in the cookery programmes or daytime TV shows that were on.

Her mother returned at six and Keira busied herself in the kitchen as her mum came into the house.

"Had a good day?" She asked and Keira shrugged non-commitally.

Mrs Lewis picked up the three envelopes from the table. One was the gas bill; she quickly put that down again. The other was advertising for something she didn't want and she held the third one in her hand for a few moments, reading the envelope, before she finally opened it.

Keira had stopped trying to pretend she was busy. She just stood there sheepishly waiting for the explosion she knew was coming.

"Well!" Exclaimed her mother at last. She stared at her daughter and Keira couldn't tell if she was angry or just confused.

"Well," she said again. "What have you been up to now, young lady?"

"I'm sorry," Keira whispered, not sure where she could start. "I just wanted to try. To see whether I could get a place. I know you don't like me dancing but I love it. It's all I want to do. I just want to be a dancer, mum."

To her shock, her mother sank slowly into a chair, the letter still in her hand. And then she began to cry.

"I'm sorry, mum. Truly I am. I didn't mean to upset you."

Keira hurried to her mother's side and put her hand on her arm, squeezing it gently. She felt the tears stinging her own eyes as her mother sniffed back her sobs and blew her nose loudly on a tissue.

"Whatever it was you did, it seems the school was impressed with you. They have offered you a place. A scholarship as well so you won't have to pay for it."

"What?"

Keira stared at her mother, trying to understand what she meant. A place? A scholarship? It must be a mistake.

"Read it," her mother said, pushing the letter into her hands.

Keira read it. She had to read it three times before it made any sort of sense. The Stageschool were indeed offering her a scholarship. Her! Keira Lewis. Not Lucy Green. It explained quite clearly what she had done but that the school considered her to have great potential and were prepared to offer her a place, nevertheless. Not only that, they had offered a full scholarship which meant everything would be paid for. She couldn't believe it. For a moment she felt light-headed and everything in the room seemed to spin, then she felt her mother guiding her into a chair and she sat down heavily, her legs no longer able to hold her up.

"Oh mum, can I go?" Her voice was barely a whisper.

"Keira, you've no idea what it's like, this dancing business. You work and work and work and very few people ever make it to the top. You end up weary, aching and injured and then you are just thrown onto the scrapheap like an old doll. It's not an easy life."

"I don't mind. I will work and work, I promise. At least let me try."

"I guess I can't do anything else really," her mum said with a sigh. "I see you will have to find out the hard way, but don't say I didn't warn you when you have bunions, knee injuries and back problems. When you're living out of a suitcase in cheap b&bs with not enough money to pay the rent let alone put food in your mouth. You'll be all washed up by the time you're thirty and no one will want to know you then."

Keira stared at her mum in surprise. "It's nothing like that at all," she said. "Colin's sister goes to a school in Manchester and she loves it. They do all sorts of dancing, not just ballet, and some of the girls have jobs while they're still at the school."

For a moment Mrs Lewis said nothing, just stared at her daughter's eager eyes and glowing expression. Then she sighed, a sound like a balloon going down slowly and she took the letter back from Keira.

"I have to fill in a form," she said. "Send it back to them. You have no idea what you are letting yourself in for but if that's what you want..."

115

"Oh thanks mum, thank you, thank you, thank you. I'll be good, I promise and I'll work very hard. I want you to be proud of me."

"I'm sure I will," she replied, with a resigned tone in her voice. "Now, let's have some tea. I need a bit of peace and a rest. I've been on my feet all day."

"I'll do it."

She wanted to dance around the kitchen but she that would annoy her mother even more so she tried her best to curb her excitement. That was about as easy as trying to catch a rainbow in a jam jar. It was amazing how one letter had totally changed her life and she had been worried all week about it arriving.

Suddenly she remembered Lucy. Had she had a letter yet and what did hers say? Was her mother cross with her? Would she be in trouble for missing her chance of a place or had they said she could try again next year? Keira hoped so, it would be good if Lucy came too because they had been friends for so long. Going to Stageschool together would be brilliant.

"Can I phone Lucy after tea?"

"If you are quick."

It was Mrs Green that answered the phone and she didn't sound very pleased when she heard who was calling.

"She's just going to have a bath," she told Keira. "You will have to be quick."

"Did you get a letter from the Stageschool today?" Keira asked.

"Yes, they said I can try again next year. Did you get in awful trouble?"

"No, not really. In fact, they offered me a place there, said I could have a scholarship and everything and my mum has agreed I can go."

"Really?"

116

For a brief moment Lucy wondered if her friend was making it all up, but what would be the point? She would get found out quickly enough if she was still at the new school in September.

"Yes. You're not cross with me, are you? For getting a place I mean. It should have been your place really."

"Well, not if I wasn't good enough. And they said I could try again next year. Sometimes I wonder if I would really like it at Stageschool. It's alright going to Miss Shelley's, her lessons are fun, but I don't know about all the other stuff. You can tell me all about it when you get there and I can see what I think. Sometimes I think it's my mum that actually wants me to go, not me."

Keira laughed. "Isn't it funny?" she said. "My mum doesn't want me to go and I've got a place."

They both started to laugh. Life was so strange sometimes that you just had to laugh!

Chapter sixteen

It was like living in a dream. Suddenly there was so much to do before September and it just didn't seem real. Instead of shopping for hockey boots and tennis rackets they now had to buy leotards and several different kinds of dance shoes as well as a very expensive uniform that could only be bought in one particular shop.

Keira saw her mother grow pale as she read the list and she felt really sorry for her. She knew it had never been easy for her mum bringing her up alone and managing the salon at the same time. Although she had always had everything she needed, and a few treats besides, Keira realised her mother must have gone without things at times in order to provide for her daughter.

She knew she had got a grant towards the uniform but guessed it wouldn't cover the cost of everything she would need.

"I'm sorry mum," Keira whispered. "I know it's a lot of money. I'll pay you back one day, when I'm grown up."

Lauren smiled faintly. "When you're rich and famous you mean? I'll hold you to that. But don't worry, the grant will help out and I have some money put away. I thought we could have a holiday later on this year, but we'll use it for the uniform instead."

Now Keira felt even more guilty. Not only was it costing a lot of money but her mum was going to miss out on the chance of a holiday too.

"I'm really sorry."

"Don't be. I know you won't let me down. It isn't what I would have wanted you to do but it's your life."

"Thanks mum."

Keira felt a tide of emotion sweep over her and she threw her arms around her mother's waist and gave her hug. She could feel tears pricking the back of her eyes but she didn't want to cry. It was hard to know what to say, her mum was giving her this chance even though she had never liked Keira dancing.

"Just do your best," her mother said, picking the list up again and pretending to study it in order to hide the tears that had filled her own eyes. Neither of them were very good at saying what they felt and preferred to hide their emotions.

"There's a lot to do," Lauren said, busying herself in the kitchen. "After tea we'll make a list then we can start buying things a few at a time. We will have to go into town. I hope we can get everything we need."

Keira wanted to rush out straight away and buy all the uniform. It was so much more exciting than the usual sort of school uniform shopping.

She studied the prospectus and imagined herself in the grey skirt and blazer, pale yellow blouse with the darker yellow and grey striped tie. She gazed at the pictures of girls in black leotards and pink shoes lined perfectly at the barre, not a hair out of place. There were girls in tunics and tap shoes; grey sweatpants, yellow t-shirts and grey hooded tops for modern dance and drama. The timetable was fascinating. Lessons started at eight-thirty and the mornings were spent in dance, drama and music. The afternoons were for academic subjects but

119

there was more choice of subjects and the classes were much smaller than Keira was used to. On Wednesday evenings there were more lessons but the subjects sounded fun; stagecraft, make-up, choreography, scripting, wardrobe. They could choose two per term and Keira tried to guess what she would like to do in her first term. It was impossible to imagine.

They did prep and private study every evening; there were hobbies and clubs that they could do at the weekend and a small amount of free time. It was organised so the first years could be doing something for most of the time thus avoiding any chance of home-sickness but there was free-time if they wanted it.

Not that Keira could imagine home-sickness, there was just too much to do and boredom wouldn't have the slightest possibility of raising its head.

And she would actually be there! Dancing in the studio, studying in the library, learning in the bright, modern classrooms, eating in the cafeteria, sleeping in one of the bedrooms that she would share with another girl from her form.

The school ran a buddying system and tried to match up girls with similar backgrounds or interests so they wouldn't be lonely. Not that Keira could imagine that either but she suddenly thought of all the friends she had known at school since she was five years old and especially Lucy. Of course she would miss her mother; it was hard to imagine her not being there when she came home from school with her news and troubles.

"I will miss you," her mother said, as if she had suddenly read Keira's mind. "Make sure you write every week."

"Of course I will and we are allowed to phone and it's only six weeks to the first half term then I will be back again."

Keira couldn't help feeling a tad guilty that she was so excited about going that she was less worried than her mother was about the approaching separation. In fact she was counting the days and had marked it off on her calendar.

In the corner of her room stood a brand new suitcase which was gradually filling up with uniform; a backpack that already boasted a pencil case and everything she needed for her school lessons but, most exciting of all, was the special holdall in which all her dance kit was lovingly waiting.

Every night, when she went to her room, she couldn't resist taking it all out and laying it across her bed, folding and refolding it, touching the softness of the leotards, folding the ribbons around her shoes and feeling the satin between her fingers, stroking the wraparound cardigan and counting the headbands, nets and pins for her hair. Then she would go to bed with the prospectus in her hand and dream that she was already there. She, Keira Lewis, at Stageschool.

The days passed. School broke up and, at the end of term assembly; Keira was called up to the front with one or two other children who had an unusual or outstanding achievement.

Katy Wilson had won a national gymnastics competition, Laura Miller was going to a special school where she would learn music and Nathan Birch was going to train to be a show jumper but Keira Lewis had won a scholarship to the Stageschool and she was going to learn how to be a dancer.

It didn't matter how many rosettes Nathan had or gold medals for Katy and she wasn't the slightest bit interested in Laura Miller and her silly clarinet. All Keira could think about was that in four weeks, then three, then two she would be leaving home and heading for a new life, an exciting time of dance and drama and dreams.

But when the morning dawned there was still a knot of excitement in her stomach. She was too nervous to eat breakfast, although her mother tried to act as if it was just a normal Saturday even she only nibbled at the toast and sipped a cup of tea as she glanced at the TV.

The weather report was good and there were no traffic problems, so Lauren was happy as they loaded the bags into the boot of the car and finally set off from the home where Keira had lived most of her life.

As the car gave a little jolt as they pulled away from the house Keira's heart gave a little jump too as she realised her life would be very different when she returned here in six weeks time.

Lauren turned on the radio and they chattered as they would do if they were heading into town on a Saturday morning. There was so much she wanted to say to her daughter as she set out on this new phase of her life but all she could think of was to make sure she did her homework and don't forget to write.

"Of course I won't," Keira replied, meaning about the letter, then laughed as she realised it had sounded like she meant she wouldn't do her homework.

Somehow that made everything better and they were able to relax as the journey continued and they neared their destination.

Stopping briefly for a burger in a fast food restaurant, although Keira knew that kind of food would be frowned upon once she started at the Stageschool, it made the treat all the more delicious as she and her mother spent their last Saturday together for several weeks.

They both felt in a lighter mood as they knew the school was only half an hour's drive away, the sun had come out and Keira felt as if she would burst as they drove into the town where the school was situated.

"Nearly there," her mother said and they realised that most of the traffic was heading in the same direction, towards the large, grey building that stood back from the road and was encircled by green lawns and several tall trees.

Keira held her breath. This was it. This was the Stageschool she had been dreaming about for so long and they were pulling up in the car park at the front of the building, along with a dozen or so other cars from which spilled swarms of equally excited children, mostly girls of about Keira's age but with one or two boys and a couple of much older girls.

They must be the Seniors. The prospectus said that sometimes senior pupils were admitted to the school if they had shown exceptional talent. Keira wondered what it must be like to be one of them. They seemed so aloof, confident and poised. Not like the first years who were all jumping about nervously and talking in high-pitched, excited voices.

She wondered who they all were. Who would she be sharing in a room with, who would become her friends, her classmates for the next year? It was a daunting prospect. Other parents were looking round apprehensively, just like hers was, and there seemed to be an entire mountain of cases piling up on the drive.

There were two women standing with clipboards by the front steps and the parents and children were steadily making their way over to them and being directed into the main hall where people were shuffling into chairs and the principal stood up at the front of the room and waited for the noise to subside.

"Welcome," she began, and silence filled the room as everyone settled down to listen to the principal's speech about the first step on the path to the rest of their lives and how it was up to them to make the most of the great opportunity that beckoned them.

Keira sat on the edge of her seat as she listened and she felt as if every word was meant just for her. This was the first step on the road ahead and, although she gave her mum a big hug after the speech had finished, the tea had been drunk and the biscuits eaten, the chats with other equally nervous parents and children were over, Keira couldn't wait to get to her new room and start to unpack her things.

She wanted to settle into her new room with her new room-mate and take that first step along the road the principal had been talking about.

Their names were called out in twos from a list and they followed another teacher upstairs to the rooms they were to share. Keira's room-mate was called Sophia and she was a very pretty little girl with her dark hair framing her elfin face.

Keira smiled at her at Sophia smiled back, a practised smile, the sort that appeared on TV adverts and it made Keira feel slightly overawed.

The room was neat and not too big and had number eleven on the door and both their names printed on a white card with a picture of a swan on.

"Now girls," the teacher, who had introduced herself as Miss Smith, said. "You can choose your own bed, unpack your cases and make yourselves at home. In two hours tea will be available in the cafeteria and then you will be shown around the school by some of the second years. There are activities for the weekend to help you get used to the place and get to know each other. If you need anything there will be staff in the hall all day. Run along now."

The two girls stood in the room, looking at each other shyly.

"I'll have this bed," Sophia said and Keira was slightly taken aback. She had expected that they would discuss it or that they would get to decide but it seemed Sophia had already made her mind up. Not that it mattered that much, both beds were identical and there were two wardrobes and two chests of drawers in the room as well as a desk and a large, easy chair by the window.

This was to be her home for the next year and she couldn't wait to put her things where she wanted them.

Sophia seemed to have the same idea and they were soon busy unpacking, chatting occasionally but it seemed strange to keep bumping into another person when she was used to having a room of her own. Well, she guessed she would get used to it and, after all, they both had the same interests and the same ambitions and dreams so they should get on well together – shouldn't they?

Keira couldn't help feeling that Sophia was just a tad bossy but she didn't mind too much. After all, she was at Stageschool now. Finally. After all that had happened she had made it and nothing was going to get in her way now, especially a bossy girl like Sophia Petit.

Chapter seventeen

The first week at Stageschool was a whirl of colours and sounds and faces for Keira. It was all new and exciting for the first years and they quickly got used to the patronising looks of the older students as they had to ask their way to yet another classroom or dance studio.

It was like a maze. The old part of the building at the front consisted of large, high-ceilinged rooms that were used for dance and drama studios. Long windows let in plenty of light and there were views out over the lawns at the front of the school. Above the studios were art rooms, rooms for costume design and a make-up studio. There were even room in what had once been the servant's quarters right up in the eaves of the house which were now sound-proofed for music practice.

An extension had been built behind the original grey stone house which now housed modern, purpose-built classrooms, a cafeteria and a well-equipped library. The basement now contained a kitchen, laundry room, several offices and a large area for storing props. They had been shown round on the first day but told that the entire basement was out of bounds for students during the term.

The boarder's rooms were on the top floor of the new wing, apart from the senior students who had separate accommodation further away from the main building.

They were lucky enough to have studio flats that they could decorate themselves and Keira wondered if she would ever make it to these illustrious heights. The seniors seemed so aloof, a completely different race as they rushed off to rehearsals and auditioned for real parts on television and stage.

Would she ever join the ranks of the seniors? There were five years to go before then and anything could happen. She might grow too tall, Keira knew dancers were only expected to be a certain height and there were few tall ballet dancers. Injuries could befall even the best dancers and promising talent sometimes failed to materialise. It was a sobering thought.

Keira was determined to do everything possible to ensure she would be the best that she could. She would practice every hour of the day, work hard at her school lessons and be as helpful as she could in order to succeed. Now that she had been given this opportunity she was determined not to fail.

There were fourteen students in Keira's class and they very soon got to know each other. Eight girls and four boys who would be spending the next year together, who came from very different backgrounds but all had the same goal in mind. They all wanted to be dancers or actors, of one type or another.

To begin with they were all getting to know their way around the building, memorising complicated timetables, overcoming shyness and homesickness and making friends.

Keira was eager to get to know the others in her class as she didn't like the idea of spending the whole year on her own, she missed Lucy and wasn't sure if she would like sharing a room with Sophia. She wasn't used to sharing a room with anyone and it seemed strange at first, especially as Sophia wasn't particularly tidy and seemed to want to take over the whole room with her clothes, books and CDs. She had already put posters up on most of the walls, Keira hadn't thought to bring any, and liked to listen to music when they were meant to be studying which made it difficult for Keira to concentrate.

Sophia had placed photos of her mother all over her desk and she wasted no time in telling everyone in the class that her mother was a famous dancer.

"You must have heard of her, she's called Marguerite Petit and she danced at Covent Garden. All the major roles, her Odette/Odile was sublime. It said so in the Dancing Times."

Keira had never heard of her, neither had most of the children in her class, although Sophia seemed to think that it showed their lack of knowledge in all things balletical. A couple of the girls decided very early on that they didn't want to be friends with Sophia and that made it difficult for Keira as she was sharing a room with her.

She didn't want to fall out with anyone but Sophia could be a bit annoying at times. Luckily, there were others in her class that she really got on with and they were starting to divide into little groups of friends. And with it only being a small class it didn't take long to get to know everyone.

There was one person she was rather in awe of, an American guy by the name of T.J who seemed very confident and an excellent dancer as well as very extrovert in everything he did. Keira couldn't help admiring him. Everyone stopped to watch whenever it was his turn to dance or sing or act and he had already had several small parts in films and on television.

Keira expected him to be really big-headed but, surprisingly he wasn't. He was a very hard worker, often getting to the class before everyone else and staying behind to go over something he wasn't happy about.

It was after one of the modern dance classes that Keira got talking to him. She had found the lesson particularly tricky, never having done modern dance before, and was just going over a few of the more complicated steps when she realised that T.J was behind her.

"You have a good line," he commented in a way that made her blush. "But you have to remember that modern dance isn't like ballet. Watch me. Dah. da da da. Dah dad ah dad ah da. Make it sharper." And he demonstrated the steps.

"Oh, I see. You make it look so easy."

"Well it's not easy. But I have been doing modern longer than I have been doing ballet. Both my parents are dancers so I danced as soon as I could stand up. How 'bout you?"

"Oh, not that long really. In fact my mother didn't want me to learn to dance at all, thinks it's a waste of time. Then I changed places with Lucy at the audition..."

"Whoa. You did what?"

"Changed places with my best friend Lucy. It was all because of the *Silver Fairy*, that's what gave us the idea."

"I think you had better start from the beginning. How about a drink in the cafeteria? I want to hear all about this."

"Ok." Suddenly Keira felt very grown-up, going to the cafeteria with T.J instead of Sophia or Ana, another girl in her class. She liked the way they could go to the cafeteria whenever they liked, there were always drinks and snacks available as well as the meals that they could choose from at meal times. It wasn't like school at all.

The food on offer was very different too as they all had to be aware of what they ate so as not to put on too much weight and still have the energy for the gruelling regime of classes.

Now Keira sat at one of the round, red-topped tables with T.J and sipped at an orange juice while she told him the whole story of her dance lessons with Miss Shelley, dancing the *Silver Fairy* in the show and then switching places with Lucy for the audition at the Stageschool.

"Well, I'll be!" T.J exclaimed in his peculiar Southern drawl. "You're quite some gal. I had every opportunity to dance, in fact it would have been hard not to with parents like mine, but you've had to do all that just to get into the place. I guess there's no stopping you when you make up your mind to something."

Keira laughed. It sounded like a compliment and it was certainly nice to have someone like T.J praising her.

"Hey, if you want any extra practice in modern just holler. I don't mind at all. You're obviously the gutsy type and I like that. Meanwhile, you could help me out with my ballet. Your technique is slightly different to mine; this RAD isn't what I learned back in the States. You could help me catch up."

"Sure." Keira found herself imitating T.J's accent unintentionally. "I don't mind at all. It will be extra practice for me as well."

"It's a deal then." He held up his hand and, for a moment Keira was confused. He couldn't want her to shake hands surely. She held up her hand too and T.J slapped his palm against hers and laughed.

He wasn't big-headed after all. He was really very nice and he was willing to learn from her as well as help her out so he couldn't be all that bad. He was also rather funny in an adult kind of way, not a jokey sort of way but he just seemed to say things in a way that made her laugh and he didn't boast about his parents like Sophia did, always going on about her mother, he just mentioned things in an off-hand kind of way so Keira hardly noticed what he had said until after he had said it.

Yes, she decided she really liked T.J and it wasn't long before they were hanging out together for most of their free time.

Then there was Leon. He was a coloured kid and seemed to have an attitude problem to begin with. Leon was a good dancer but didn't like to join in with the others. He even sat on his own in the cafeteria and refused any attempts to be drawn in with the groups that sat around at break time. Eventually they gave up asking him but Keira couldn't help feeling a bit sorry for him. He was always the odd one out.

But perhaps he liked it like that. It wasn't as if he was the only coloured kid in the school. Keira had noticed a Chinese girl in the seniors, very pretty and dainty with large almond eyes, and another dark-skinned boy who sang in a group with two other boys and a skinny girl with long blond hair.

There was also a French boy called Claude and a Spanish girl, Maria Gomez, who had a part in a show that meant she had to go to rehearsals every afternoon. Keira couldn't understand why Leon seemed to prefer to keep away from everybody when part of the fun of being at the Stageschool was the fact that they all had the same ambitions and goals. They might come from different backgrounds, have different experiences but one bond drew them all together, the love of dance and all things theatrical.

It didn't take long for any conversation to be turned to the favourite theme. Even the school lessons seemed to lead to discussions of their favourite dancers, the latest ballet they had seen, the shows they had appeared in, the costumes they wore, the music they loved. It was why they were here, what drew them together and everyone except Leon wanted to belong to the clique, be part of the crowd, one of the team.

A girl named Ruby had also become Keira's particular friend and the two of them had similar tastes in most things. They even enjoyed the same lessons and sat next to each other in class. Ruby, unlike Keira, had several brothers and sisters. An elder sister, who went to a prestigious music school, played three different instruments and was practically a child prodigy. Her two brothers were exceptionally clever, attending a private school were they were learning lessons well in advance of their age group, and even her youngest sister, Fifi, was showing signs of being musically gifted and had won a national talent show resulting in a recording contract.

As half term approached school had settled into a regular routine. The first years had quickly thrown off any hint of homesickness and could find their way around the building without a second thought.

"I don't know what all the fuss was about," Ruby declared as they made their way to a history lesson with Mr Rogers. "It's like we've been here forever."

"And I hope we never have to leave," Keira added.

132

"Well, I don't know about that. Won't it be exciting when we get proper parts in real shows? I'm going to be in the West End." She spoke with conviction. Something Keira had found hard to accept at first was the absolute confidence of some of the students but she was now learning the importance of believing in herself. There was no room for doubt in the minds of the dancers.

"In order to achieve they had to believe", was the motto of the school and Keira understood the reality of it now. She was loving every minute of being here. It all made it so real; the dance lessons, history of the theatre, choreography lessons, musicality, make-up, costumes. They were part of a different world now. Every minute of the day was taken up with learning how to dance, sing and act and there wasn't one person there that didn't follow the dream, no matter what it took, they would reach their star.

Apart from Leon, that is.

Keira just couldn't figure him out or why he was at the Stageschool at all when he didn't seem to want to be part of anything.

Chapter eighteen

Half term had caught them all unawares. They had been enjoying their first term at the Stageschool so much that it was almost a disappointment to realise that they had to go home tomorrow. Like being told to put down a book just as the interesting part had been reached in order to go to the table. Or having to miss the end of a television programme because it was time for bed.

That was how Keira felt as she packed away her books at the end of the afternoon and realised there was no school for a whole week. No dancing, no drama, not even any lessons! Despite the fact she had written to her mother every week, and to Lucy slightly less often, it seemed strange to think that she was actually going to see them again.

Six weeks at Stageschool had turned her into a different person. She was aware that she was not the Keira who had left home at the beginning of September. Although she appeared more confident in many ways she had also come to realise just how far from her goal she was and how hard she would have to work over the next five years to get any where near where she wanted to be.

Compared to most in her class she was way behind and, if it wasn't for the extra help she was getting from T.J and the encouragement of Ruby, she might be feeling totally demoralised by now.

"How was it?" Lucy asked. "Tell me all about it. Have you made loads of friends? What are the teachers like?"

"Woa. One question at a time," Keira said with a laugh. "I love it. I have made friends with a girl called Ruby and an American guy called T.J, he's really cool."

"Wow! An American. How awesome. What's he like?"

Keira had worried that Lucy might feel jealous that she was at Stageschool now instead of her but she didn't seem at all resentful. Just really interested.

"He's funny and nice and really good looking. All the girls are jealous, even the older ones, because we are friends but it's not like that, well, you know what I mean. We are just like mates. And Ruby's really nice too. Just ordinary. Not big-headed like Sophia because her mum *used* to be a dancer. No one has even heard of her. But T.J's parents are both famous in the States but he doesn't go on about it all the time."

"You are so lucky," Lucy said. "It's nothing like normal school. Just French and History and Maths. Hockey on freezing cold days and tennis when it's too hot. I am envious of you, even though it was my idea to change places, but I'm not sure it's what I want. I just know I would like to do something different, more exciting."

"Well, what do you like? At school I mean. And you still have lessons with Miss Shelley."

"Oh yes. And I'm not sure I would like to go to Stageschool but when I'm sat in a Maths lesson with Mr Burgess droning on about fractions and equations, I just wish I was anywhere else."

"I know what you mean. And we still do ordinary lessons. Every afternoon. And we have to work hard because, if we don't pass our exams we could be thrown out of the school, no matter how good we are at dance. And we have to improve in all the dance classes and not get injured or grow too tall. It's quite a scary thought sometime."

"Poor you," Lucy said, in a joking kind of way that meant she didn't feel sorry for her friend at all. "What about your mum? Is she ok with it all now?"

"Well, kind of. She asks how I'm getting on and everything but I still think she would rather I was somewhere else. It's almost like she's waiting for something to go wrong and then she can say 'I told you so.'"

"I wonder why she hates it so much."

"She never really says. When I ask she changes the subject as quickly as possible and just says she hopes I'm happy, or something like that. What about your mum? Is she still cross with me?"

"No. I don't think so. Not now. She can see I'm not upset about you going instead so she must realise it wasn't that important to me. I wouldn't have suggested it if I really wanted to go, anyway."

"I hope you find something you want to do. Do you still see Colin?"

"Not really. He goes to the Grammar School now, the one by the river, posh uniform and everything. But then he always was a brainbox. I saw him with his sister the other day and they asked how you are getting on. Debra's got a part in some children's TV series. Can't remember what it's called but it will be out at Christmas, she said."

"How exciting."

"That's what I thought. And it made me realise how boring my life is."

"You will find something, I know you will. Cheer up."

"I hope so. Anyway, there's plenty of time. Another five years of school at least and mum's going on about college and Uni. Not that I'm clever enough for that."

Keira didn't want Lucy getting gloomy again. "Shall we do something this week? Go to the pictures or something? Go into town and have a pizza?"

"Yeah, that would be great. What about Tuesday? My dad could take us."

"Ok. Tuesday's fine. I can't wait."

It felt strange walking around her old town again. Everything seemed to have shrunk. Keira just couldn't explain it but her six weeks away seemed to have changed everything.

Was it her that had changed? The town looked the same; the same shops, the library had the same books, she had actually read most of them, but everything seemed so small, dull, insignificant.

Lucy chatted away as if nothing had happened but Keira knew it was all different. Even Lucy seemed so much younger, more childish and Keira knew it was because she had been living away from home. Living with people whose first thought was always about their dancing and where everything else came a poor second. Children they may be, but they already understood the meaning of dedication, commitment, ambition.

They knew that, in order to achieve they had to work hard, suffer sore toes and tired limbs, push themselves to the absolute limit of their endurance and then one step further. It wasn't an easy life and they had had to give up much of what ordinary children enjoy; trips to burger bars, late nights, and the luxury of lie-ins and lazy indulgence.

That's what made everything seem different to Keira. A whole new perspective of life that had altered everything and even made the way she perceived Lucy, her friend for many years, in a totally different light.

Lucy had no discipline. She could eat what she liked and not have to worry about it because the dance lessons with Miss Shelley did not call for the same commitment as life at the Stageschool did.

Sadly, Keira realised she had grown apart from her one-time best friend. Not that she wanted to rub it in when it was all due to Lucy that she had gone to the Stageschool in the first place. But she felt like they were now in different worlds and there was no bridge to cross from one to the other. Even Lucy's interest in ballet was not enough, if anything it made the gap wider.

Keira tried her best. She sat through a mediocre film, went to the pizza parlour and only ate salad, tried not to talk about the Stageschool all the time and forced herself to think about subjects other than ballet. But it was hard. And she realised that she couldn't wait to get back to school, something that had never happened before, and was glad when the week was over.

This time any feelings of homesickness lasted less than a day. As soon as she was dropped off at the Stageschool she couldn't wait to get back to her room and put her things away. The only fly in the ointment was the fact that she had to share with Sophia, who was just as boastful as ever and couldn't wait to tell everyone that she had been to the ballet with her mother *and* gone backstage to meet the principal dancers.

Keira felt a prickle of annoyance and was quite glad to escape to the *chill out* room to see if any of the others were back. Unfortunately, the only person from her class was Leon and she didn't think he would be very chatty. She was just about to turn round and walk out when something made her change her mind.

"Hi," she said, walking over to the sofa where Leon was reading a magazine. "Did you have a good half-term?"

Leon glanced up briefly, grunted and returned to the magazine.

Keira was annoyed. There was no need to be rude. He could at least answer her. Before she had realised what she was doing, Keira had sat down beside Leon on the sofa. Now what was she going to do? She couldn't think of anything to say to him.

He looked up in surprise, not used to anyone invading his space he glared at Keira.

"What do you want?"

"There's no need to be rude. Why are you always like that? We are all here for the same thing, to learn to dance. I don't know what's wrong with you but no one will want to be friends with you if you carry on like that."

For once Leon was shocked. No one had spoken to him like that before. And who was she? This posh girl, probably loads of money and been dancing since she was a baby.

"You don't know what you're talking about." Leon muttered. "Leave me alone."

"Okay," Keira agreed, getting up from the sofa. "But don't say I didn't warn you, no one will like you if you carry on like that." And she stormed away before Leon had chance to reply.

She didn't know who was worse, sulky Leon or big-headed Sophia. Luckily, she bumped into Ruby and Millie on their way to the cafeteria so she decided to join them. They shared a room and seemed to be becoming quite good friends now. Arm in arm, they

139

were practically like sisters and Keira envied them. It would be nice to have someone like that to share a room with, someone she could gossip to like she used to with Lucy. It was a good thing that everyone at Stageschool wasn't like Sophia or Leon.

Most were really nice. Even the boys, and she had become quite friendly with T.J . Dominic she wasn't quite sure of he seemed terribly posh and someone said he had a very rich family but Matty was okay, very lively and wanting to be friends with everyone. He was rapidly gaining a reputation as the class joker and no one could say anything bad about Matty.

With his sandy hair and freckles there was an appealing quality about Matty that reminded Keira of a lost puppy. Everyone wanted to take care of him. Even the teachers seemed to have a soft spot for Matty Weston and he was favourite in most of his classes.

Except, of course, for Madame. Madame Alicia Lewinsky had no favourites. She rarely took the juniors for classes anyway but, a couple of weeks after half term, it was announced that she would be taking them for one lesson during the week. Nobody knew which one but there was a heightened feeling of excitement in the class each time they entered the studio, wondering if it would be her taking the class today.

On Thursday they entered as usual to find Mrs Fox standing by the piano discussing the music for the lesson. The children lined up at the barre and waited for the class to begin. No one heard the door open behind them. They were all focusing their thoughts as they had been taught to do at the beginning of the lesson, imaging every bone in their spine in a perfect line, their feet neatly turned out at the ankle, arms relaxed by their side waiting for the first instruction, the first note of music that would lift them from their daily lives to another plane where they were transformed into completely different creatures; sylph-like, fairy folk, full of grace and perfect in line and poise.

A gentle tapping sound caught their attention and Mrs Fox sank into a graceful curtsey. Reflected in the mirror behind her the class caught sight of the legendary Madame, dressed entirely in black with a silk scarf swathed around her swan-like neck and a silver-tipped cane in her hand.

"Good morning, class."

"Good morning, Madame." There was a slight rustle as the girls bobbed their curtsies; the boys bent their heads in a bow.

"Thank you, Mrs Fox. If you would be so kind, I will take the class today."

Mrs Fox dropped another curtsey and hurried from the room, sending the class a pleading look as she left, as if to say, "please don't let me down."

A discernable silence filled the room. Not a shuffle or mutter, not a cough or fidget was heard as everyone strove to be the very best under Madame's watchful eye.

Too late Millie wished she had put extra hair grips in her notoriously unruly frizz. Ruby wished she had washed her tights last night and Polly Wilson remembered that she still had her earrings in, a definite taboo in any dance class, let alone Madame Lewinsky's ballet class. Polly hoped she wouldn't notice.

"Now, we will begin. Pliés everyone, first position and..."

A ripple of nervous anticipation ran around the class like a sigh. Everyone felt it, like a current of electricity it passed from one to the other. Even Leon seemed to be affected by it as he stood up straighter than he ever had before and turned his knees out over his toes with exact precision.

Madame walked up and down between the rows of eager students. Rarely speaking, occasionally pausing beside a pupil to correct a position with a touch of her hand or stick.

Twice she stopped by Keira and Keira felt her heart beat faster. Had she done something wrong? Was her head out of line? Her leg not turned out enough? Her back not straight enough? She desperately hoped not. How awful to make a mistake in front of Madame herself.

"Thank you, class. May I remind you that no jewellery is to be worn to classes and students are expected to look immaculate at all times? Nothing less than perfection will do."

As the class came to an end they were instructed to say their names as they made their curtsey or bow. Starting at the front, Polly was the first and she actually wobbled as she stepped up before Madame. How awful!

Keira was fourth and she hardly dare breathe as she whispered her name.

"Keira Lewis."

Raising her eyes she found Madame staring at her with that piercing gaze that seemed to know exactly what she was thinking.

A slight incline of her head as Keira moved on and Sophia took her place, sweeping a deep curtsey and over-affected twirl of her hand, just what Madame *didn't* like.

They all hurried to the changing room where they burst out into excited chatter, relief engulfing them.

"Did you see how Polly wobbled?" Sophia laughed. "And Millie's glissades were like glue." She imitated someone trying to glide through a patch of glue, feet sticking to the floor instead of gliding gracefully.

"Shut up, Sophia. You weren't perfect."

"At least I wasn't wearing earrings or grubby tights. You might as well have been chewing gum in Madame's class. How unprofessional."

"What do you know? Just 'cos your mother was in the corps de ballet of some third rate company."

"How dare you? My mother was a famous dancer, I'll have you know, she danced for the Queen at Covent Garden."

"Ladies, ladies. Hurry along. You have another class to go to."

It was Mrs Fox and she flapped her arms around, trying to hurry them along.

"Sorry, miss."

"I hope you didn't let me down today."

"No, miss."

"Good. I will see you all tomorrow. I'm sure Madame will have only good reports of you all."

"Yes, miss." And they changed quickly, hurrying off to the modern jazz class that followed after a short morning break.

I hope Madame has a good report of me, Keira thought, as she sipped a glass of juice in the cafeteria. I really hope she does.

Chapter nineteen

Keira would have been surprised to know that Madame was thinking of her at exactly that same moment. Sitting alone in her office she was staring wistfully out of the window, a far-off expression on her face. To her right stood a heavy wooden bookcase filled with books about dance and several, silver-framed photographs were placed along the top.

One, in black and white, showed herself as a young woman dancing Odette in *Swan Lake.* Another showed a young boy posed in relaxed mode against a barre, his black hair swept back in classical style and wearing black tights and a white t-shirt. The third showed the same boy, now a young man, executing a grand jétè across the stage. He appeared to be floating, caught as he was in mid-flight.

It was this that had caught her eye and she sighed, for this was her son, now dead and a pain tugged at her heart as she thought of him. David. Her beloved.

For a moment a tear froze in the corner of her eye and she forced her thoughts back to the present day. That child, that Keira Lewis, there was something about her. She would ask for her records, find out what she could about her. Meanwhile, there was no time for reverie. She had a school to run, an academy that was second to none in the area and she was determined to keep it that way. Many of her students had gone on to achieve great things, careers on the stage, television and in films. Selena Thompson had gone on to join the Scottish Ballet's touring company and had even danced Giselle. She was a name to watch. Just occasionally Madame picked out someone with exceptional promise at a young age. They didn't always go on to flower but today she had seen just such a student and she was determined to keep an eye on her. She was sure that Keira Lewis was another such as Selena.

That reminded her. Where were those files?

The excitement of Madame's class lasted until the end of the week, then another piece of news broke the spell and it was Matty who brought the information as they were waiting to go into history on a Friday afternoon.

"Have you heard about Leon?" There was concern on his freckled face.

"No, why?" Keira hadn't been all that fond of Leon since their encounter in the *chill out* room, when she had tried to make friends with him and failed.

"Apparently his mother died. She had been ill for some time. I heard one of the secretaries telling Mrs Penny that arrangements had to be made for him to go home for the funeral."

"Oh!"

A shocked silence followed this announcement and everyone realised that they hadn't seen Leon all day. The fact that he kept himself to himself most of the time meant that he could be easily overlooked. No wonder he had been less than friendly, Keira thought. But it wasn't their fault, if they didn't know there was nothing they could do about it, was there?

Nevertheless, she couldn't help feeling a twinge of guilt. How would she feel if her mother was seriously ill? Probably not much like making friends with

145

anyone. As it was, she had grown up without a father around and that had been bad enough. What must it be like to lose your mother? Keira didn't even want to think about that.

One or two people shifted uncomfortably, realising that they hadn't always been that nice to Leon, but then, he had always warded off any attempts to join in with everyone else.

"Perhaps we should do something," Millie said. "You know, send a card, collect some money. Buy flowers."

"Why would he want flowers?" Sophia asked. "That's just silly."

"No, it isn't. It just shows you are thinking about him."

"Well, I think a card," Dominic put in. "From all of us. I'll ask my mother if you like. She knows about that sort of thing."

"Okay," they all agreed. Relieved that someone seemed to know what to do. "We will all put in some money. You can get the card, Nic. We will ask Mrs Penny about where to send it to."

There was a general feeling of relief throughout the class. They had done all they could. No one could expect them to do anymore and Leon couldn't complain that no one had thought about him. They left history with a collective saintly aura and were quick to do as they promised, raid their purses and savings for money to buy something to express their concern for their classmate.

When Leon returned there was an atmosphere of hushed uncertainty whenever he was around as no one knew quite what to say to him. It was Matty with his kindly concern, who went over to him at the beginning of the modern dance class and tapped him briefly on the shoulder.

"Hey, we are all sorry to hear about your mother."

"Thanks," Leon mumbled. "And thanks guys, for the card an' stuff."

He shuffled uncomfortably on his feet and everyone was aware of the silence that filled the room. A sudden tap caught their attention and they all turned, relieved that the moment was over, glad to immerse themselves in the rhythm and the familiar steps of the dance class.

Miss Stevenson was determined to work their socks off. There was no time for self pity from any of them and they all seemed to want to put an extra effort into everything they did.

By the end of the session they were aching in every muscle, toes were bruised and egos shattered. They limped out of the class and collapsed en masse in a heap on the changing room floor.

"What's gotten into old Stevie today?" T.J gasped. "Do you think her boyfriend dumped her?"

"Whatever it was, she didn't need to take it out on us," Nic replied, gulping down water from a plastic bottle. Sweat was standing out on his forehead in glistening droplets and he wiped them away with the back of his hand.

Leon sat on the bench, his head in his hands and Matty lay stretched out on the floor, unable to move.

The girls, in their side of the room, were equally exhausted, changing in unnatural silence, the usual chatter and banter forgotten as they eased their aching joints out of tunics and dance shoes.

"Thank goodness it's theatre next," Millie managed to say. "I couldn't cope with another class like that."

Wearily they made their way to the cafeteria for drinks, piling around a couple of tables with their drinks in front of them. Even Leon was too worn out to bother about finding somewhere else to sit and slumped into a seat between Matty and Sophia.

147

All differences seemed to be forgotten as they huddled together for camaraderie.

"I don't know how we will cope with a real performance," Polly said. "Imagine doing that night after night."

Chloe groaned. "I will never walk again," she said. "I'm sure she picked on me on purpose."

"She certainly seemed to have it in for us today," Keira agreed. "Let's hope Monsieur Raymond is in a better mood."

"Oh, he's a pussycat," Millie said.

"Only 'cos you're his favourite, Miss Millie," Ruby said with a laugh. "Come on, it can't be any worse than Stevie."

"No, I guess not. Come on guys; let's show them what we're made of." T.J picked up his carton and took it over to the trolley, followed reluctantly by the rest of the group they made their way to the theatre in the old part of the school.

Keira loved the place. There was a hint of magic in the air and it reminded her of why she was here in the first place. Pausing by the door she took in a deep breath, the smell of polish assailed her, a deep, musky smell of velvet curtains and plush seats.

A hush hung over the place too, an expectancy that something was about to happen, the audience poised on the edge of their seats, the conductor raising his batten and the actors in the wings waiting to come alive. It was a wonderful place.

"Ah, mes petites," Monsieur Raymond cooed as he entered the theatre, sweeping his right arm round in an affected manner. Short and swarthy and dressed in swirling garments he was every inch the showman.

"Tout le monde, l'attention. Nous allons commencer."

It was improvisation and they were put into pairs. Keira found herself paired with Leon and she was worried about what to say to him, especially after his previous rebuff over her attempts to befriend him.

Theatre was a very absorbing lesson. Despite their various aches and pains they were soon involved with their roles. For a moment Keira felt uncomfortable. Should she say anything to Leon or should she just carry on as if it were a normal lesson? But then, he did seem to be making more of an effort to join in with them so maybe she should say something to him. Only what, she didn't know.

They were improvising a role in which they had to reverse the characters they would normally play. To her dismay Keira realised that Leon was expected to play the mother and she the son. Oh no, how would he feel? Didn't Monsieur Raymond know what had just happened? Should she say something to him and get him to change their characters to different ones?

Leon began the role-play valiantly. He had read the instructions and wavered for a moment, then the professional spirit had overcome him and he battled on for the first ten minutes. Keira noticed him begin to falter, his words wavered, his lip quivered and he fought to keep the tears from filling his eyes. Despite his earlier rebuff, Keira couldn't help a feeling of sympathy squeezing her heart as she noticed the tough guy force back the tears.

"Hey, it's okay," Keira whispered. "We don't have to do this, I will ask Monsieur Raymond to change our roles."

"No," Leon snapped. "I can do it." For a few moments he struggled with his emotions. "I'm fine. Thank you," he added in a softer tone. Meeting Keira's eye he managed a smile. "Thank you."

Keira smiled back. "That's ok."

What could she say to him? She had grown up without a father there, but then she had never met him and losing a mother who had brought you up was far worse. Poor Leon. She could sense that he didn't want sympathy; the best thing would be to just carry on as usual and let Leon concentrate on the class. That would be the best way forward.

Leon, through sheer strength of character, was able to get through the class, and the following one, and the one after that. Maybe he could sense his classmates' silent support but he managed to carry on until the end of the day.

By the time the bell had rung after the last lesson he felt exhausted, mentally and physically, and made his way to the cafeteria where he sank down into one of the comfortable armchairs in the corner. Closing his eyes he took deep breaths, momentarily giving in to a feeling of melancholy.

He was the eldest in his family, followed by four younger sisters, and now his father was left to bring them up on his own. The family would struggle for money, his father worked as a mechanic, and it seemed unfair that he should carry on at the Stageschool. But it was his dream, always had been, and his way of escape from the council estate where he had grown up.

He was just wondering whether to get himself something to eat from the counter when he saw Keira and Ruby enter the room. Oh no, the last thing he wanted right now was company. He hoped they hadn't seen him. They were getting drinks from the counter and it looked like they were coming over. His first instinct was to growl at them to go away; he wanted to be left alone. Then he remembered the card and decided he had at least better try to be polite to them.

"Hi, Leon. How are you?"

It was a stupid question anyway. How did they think he was?

He shrugged.

"Look, we all really are sorry about what happened. If there was something to do to help, we would do."

What could they do? There was no one to bring his mother back. No one to look after his little sisters, no one to pay the bills when his dad had time off work.

"Nothing really." He folded his arms and stared resolutely into space.

"Well, if there is," Keira began. "Let us know. I lost my father when I was a baby." It wasn't something she often talked about but it seemed an appropriate thing to say, just at that moment.

"I didn't know that," Ruby chipped in.

"I hardly remember him," Keira put in as way of an apology to Leon, not wanting him to think she was asking for sympathy in any way.

"It's hardly the same then, is it?" Leon replied tersely.

"No, but I just wanted you to be aware that you weren't the only one with problems of some kind." Keira's patience was wearing thin, she wanted to help him but he just wasn't being responsive at all.

"I bet you don't have four little sisters to worry about. And I might have to leave the Stageschool now; my dad won't be able to afford to pay for it."

"Oh!" Both girls exclaimed at once. Leaving the Stageschool was possibly the worst thing any of them could imagine, after losing a parent of course.

"But there are grants and things," Keira put in, remembering that she had had certain things paid for her. "Couldn't you apply for something like that?"

"My dad said he don't want no charity," Leon replied stubbornly. "And there's not just me to think of, there's me sisters too. It's not fair on them if all the money is spent on me being here."

Keira actually thought it was quite nice that Leon should think about his sisters. Although to her, her dancing would always come first and any sisters she may have had would have had no more than a passing thought.

"There must be something we can do," she said, not wanting to be beaten. "There must be some way we can help Leon stay at the Stageschool. He's too good a dancer for us to lose."

"Like what?" Ruby asked.

Leon stared at the two girls suspiciously. What were they planning now?

Chapter twenty

It was T.J that came up with the idea.

"Hey, why don't we have a fundraising? We do it a lot in the States."

"What's that?" Ruby asked.

A small group of them were sat in the cafeteria on a rainy Saturday afternoon. Millie and Chloe Taylor had gone to the library but Keira had decided to stay behind as she wasn't feeling too well, a bit snuffly and headachy, besides she hadn't finished the book she was reading on Margot Fonteyn so she didn't need to change it just yet.

Matty, Leon and Nic had gone swimming and Chloe Brown had gone on a day out with her family who were down from Lancashire visiting for a few days. Polly, Sophia and Ana were rehearsing for a pantomime that was taking place in the Grand Plaza, much to the envy of the rest of the class.

The remainder of the class, with not much to do on a Saturday afternoon, were mooching around in the cafeteria and trying not to look bored in case any passing teachers roped them in for something they didn't want to do.

There was always something. Picking up litter, showing prospective parents and their hopeful offspring round, running various errands, to cleaning all the whiteboards in the building. A task Keira had once ended up doing as she had unwittingly yawned as Mrs White walked past.

That's why they were skulking in the cafeteria, as far away from any stray staff members as possible. Not that many of them ever hung around the school at the weekend. Who could blame them? They had their own families to see to, their own tasks to do, those that were on duty and occasionally they even disappeared to do exciting things, like appear in a ballet or on television. Lucky Miss Stevenson had danced in Coppelia with a touring company for four months and Monsieur Raymond had appeared in a TV programme about famous choreographers.

"A fundraiser," T.J explained slowly, as if he were talking to half-wits. "Is where you raise funds. You bake cookies and sell them, that kind of thing."

"We would have to bake a lot of cookies to keep Leon at the Stageschool," Keira said, unconvinced.

T.J sighed heavily. "Really, you Brits! It doesn't have to be cookies. It doesn't have to be baking at all. We could do anything to raise money and use it to help Leon."

"Like what?"

"Isn't it obvious? We are all dancers! We put on a show and the money raised goes to Leon."

"Would we be allowed?" Ruby asked.

"Would Leon like that?" Keira said at the same time. "He said his father doesn't want charity."

"It won't be charity, not if he's involved with the show. Soccer stars do it and raise money for injured players. Like a benefit match."

"Well, that might be okay then. We would have to ask Leon what he thinks. And find out if we are allowed to do it."

"Don't see why not," Keira said. The idea was starting to grow on her. "There's usually a show at the end of term anyway. We could at least ask."

"Who would we ask?"

"It would have to be Madame, I suppose. We will have to ask her secretary if we can see her."

"We?" Ruby said. "It was T.J's idea. He should go and ask her."

"I don't mind," T.J replied. "But what about Keira? You can come too, can't you?"

"I suppose so. Let's get some more ideas, jot down a few things. It will look better like that."

"You're right. We will have a class meeting, tomorrow, straight after breakfast. Get everyone involved and write out a proper plan. Then we will make an appointment to see Madame."

"Agreed."

The suggestion was greeted with various degrees of enthusiasm from the rest of the class. Leon was most reluctant at first, but when it was explained that he would be involved in it, they wouldn't be doing it *for* him but *with* him he started to warm to the idea.

"It could be fun," Matty said. "Putting on a whole show by ourselves. We all have our favourite dances. Keira, Sophia and Nic are really good at ballet. I could do something comic, Ana's brilliant at folk dancing, that Spanish dance you did last week was amazing. T.J and Leon could do something modern. Polly can sing."

"I could do something from Shakespeare," Nic said. "Maybe Hamlet. Chloe, you could do Ophelia."

The enthusiasm was catching. Soon they were all coming up with suggestions of their own. Keira wrote it all down, hastily scribbling, then crossing things out until she had an entire programme set out.

"This looks really good," Leon said. "What about costumes?"

"We can do that too," Millie said. "It'll be fun. We can make some, borrow some, maybe buy a few things. My mum used to make theatrical costumes; she's always got loads of stuff lying around the house. Used to drive my dad mad. I'm sure there's stuff we could use. Shall I ask?"

"Yes, that would be great. Ruby could do the make-up. You came top in that last term."

"I would love to."

"So, do you think it will work?" Keira asked.

"Yes! Yes! Yes!" They all shouted at once.

"Keira and I will go to see Madam then," T.J said. "First thing tomorrow."

Keira spent the rest of the day writing up the notes, setting it out in a way that made sense and looked more professional. A cast list, the order of performance, ideas for costumes, music, sets and lighting. She showed it to the others on Sunday evening as they watched television in the *chill out* room and they were all impressed.

"Madame will just have to say yes when she sees this. That's amazing, Keira."

"Thanks. T.J helped too."

Straight after breakfast the following day they went to Madame's office where Miss Hulbert sat, a formidable character at the best of times but an absolute dragon when they told her they wanted to see Madame.

"You want to see Madame? Why?"

"We have an idea for a show. It's a fundraiser, to help Leon stay at the Stageschool."

"Leon?"

"Yes, Leon Knight. In the first year. His mother died and he doesn't think he will be able to stay on but we

156

thought, if we all raised some money, then we could help pay for the fees." Keira could hear herself gabbling but she didn't know how to stop. Miss Hulbert would think she was totally thick now.

She eyed the two first years in front of her. Eager expressions on their faces. She was used to ballet students by now but there was something about these two, a freshness, an enthusiasm that she liked.

Raising her eyebrows slightly, her grey eyes gazed through her steel-framed spectacles.

"I will check in the diary. Madame has a fifteen minute slot at ten-fifteen, if you can come back then. What are your names?"

"Keira Lewis and T.J Smith. Thank you."

They arrived promptly at quarter past ten, straight from the ballet class. Keira had slipped a wrap over the top of her leotard and T.J had a huge, baggy sweater over his leggings and white, t-shirt. They hadn't even changed out of their ballet shoes and Keira was aware that her face was flushed and her hair sleeked back with sweat. T.J's blond hair was swept back out of his blue eyes and his face was tanned from the time he spent out in the sun. He was very athletic looking and it was hard to imagine him as a dancer. Taller than Keira, he stood by her side and she drew confidence from him. She almost felt like she wanted to hold his hand as they waited to be called into Madame's office.

The intercom buzzed.

"You can go in now," Miss Hulbert said.

T.J winked at Keira.

"It's fine," he said.

They stepped into Madame's office. It was sparsely furnished but everything had an elegance about it, the carpet was luxurious and Keira felt her feet sinking into it. A large desk faced them and Madame was seated behind it. Her hair drawn back into a severe bun, her piercing eyes taking in the two figures in front of her. Something made Keira curtsey; it seemed the right thing to do in front of Madame. T.J gave a slight bow then they both approached the desk.

"Well," Madame said, her voice steady and firm. "Thomas Smith and Keira Lewis?"

"Yes, Madame."

"What is it you want to see me about?"

"It's about Leon Knight," T.J began. He was more confident about speaking to adults so they had agreed he would start and then Keira would show her the plans they had made.

T.J repeated the story about Leon's mother and their idea for a fund raising.

"And Leon knows about this?"

"Yes, he wants to help. Everyone in the class wants to help. We are all good at something and we have come up with a plan for the show. Keira will explain."

"Ah! Keira Lewis. Yes, I remember you."

Madame looked at the slight girl in front of her, her fair hair tied up in a bun from which a single strand had escaped and twirled down her left cheek. Her eyes were eager, her expression frank, open, honest. A pretty girl, very pretty, talented too. Madame had picked her out from the ballet class she had taken. And then she had looked up her records and what she had read had brought a strange lump to her throat, her hand to her head she had sat in silence for several minutes before returning the folder to the cabinet where it belonged.

Now she was here in front of her. This child. Madame Lewinski found it hard to meet her eyes so she concentrated on the folder in her hand.

"This is what we thought," Keira said, placing the folder on the table. Madame opened it and flipped through the pages.

"You want to put on a show, do everything yourselves, the first years? And raise money so Leon Knight can stay at the school?"

"Yes, Madame."

For a few moments Madame studied the folder in front of her.

"When were you planning to do this show?"

"At the end of term."

"When will you find time to rehearse? You won't be able to miss any of your normal lessons."

"At the weekends. And evenings. We really want to do this."

"I see. Yes, I like the idea. Somewhat ambitious, a whole show. I would like to see what you can do. You have my permission to go ahead. As long as it doesn't interfere with your other lessons. I will discuss with Monsieur Raymond about use of the theatre and arrange a date for the concert. I will be very interested to see what you can do, Keira and Thomas."

"Thank you, Madame. Oh, thank you."

"Now off to your next lesson."

"Yes, Madame." Keira curtsied again, picked up the folder and they hurried from the room. Excited that they could begin planning the show at once with the rest of the class.

"I didn't know your name was Thomas," Keira said to T.J.

"Thomas James, to be precise. But I prefer T.J. more of a ring to it don't you think?"

"I guess so," Keira said with a laugh and they hurried to the changing rooms to get changed for the tap lesson next.

159

Madame, meanwhile, hadn't moved from her chair. She was staring at the photographs on the shelf. The one of her son as a young man. An earnest expression on his face, an openness in his eyes that she had always found endearing, and she felt tears prickling the back of her eyelids. Pulling a dainty lace handkerchief from her pocket she dabbed her eyes.

Oh David, she thought, if only you were here now. You would be so proud. And she picked up her phone to speak to Monsieur Raymond about the theatre.

Keira was so excited she was jumping up and down as she told the news to the rest of the class.

"It was amazing. We actually spoke to Madame, she looked at my folder. She said she would like to see what we can do. We have to rehearse in our own time. It will be great fun. When can we start?"

"I will draw up a schedule," T.J said. "I will have to find out which rooms are empty. We will need a studio for the dance rehearsals. Nic, you can sort out the Shakespeare. Everyone can do their own choreography and we will get together in a couple of weeks to run through things together. Millie, can you start designing the costumes so we know what we need?"

"Yes, no problem. I will need everyone's sizes and then I can see what we have here already and what my mum might be able to lend us."

"I will need to start practising hair and make-up," Ruby said. "What about lunch times? There's plenty of time. Keira and Sophia, you two first. Twelve o'clock today. Your make-up is easy."

"Okay, we'll see you later. In the studio."

"That's great."

The teachers were quick to notice a difference in the first years. They were bubbling over with excitement.

"What has got into them?" Miss Stevenson asked as she sat in the staff room sipping a well-earned cup of tea.

"I don't know but I hope it continues. They are working twice as hard as usual."

"It's the show," Monsieur Raymond said. "Haven't you heard? Madame has agreed for them to put on a show at the end of term. A kind of benefit performance for Leon Knight whose mother died so that he can stay on at school."

"Really? That's a nice idea. Couldn't Madame have arranged a grant?"

"Yes, I think she was going to but she liked the fact the students all wanted to help so she let them do it. She thought it would be interesting to see what they could do on their own as well. She seems quite keen on the whole thing."

"Ah, oui. Ils semblent un bon groupe, j'espère qu'ils font de bien. They seem a good bunch. I hope they do well. Ah bien!"

Monsieur Raymond picked up a magazine from the coffee table and began flicking through it idly while he sipped a cup of strong coffee.

Soon the whole school knew about the show. There were even offers of help and one or two that wanted to take part. But it was not allowed.

"Strictly first years," T.J said, but he was enjoying the attention it brought to him and the whole class were enjoying the status that seemed to have come to them through the organising of the show.

Even Leon's story had raised a considerable amount of sympathy, but of the right type so he wasn't offended in any way and people seemed to want to help out as much as they could.

It was quite an exciting time for all concerned, getting ready for the show. Not that there weren't one or two little mishaps of course. And the occasional squabble between the students but T.J had become the official organiser of the event and his word became law. Everyone began to respect that he had a real talent for the whole thing, even the teachers had nothing but praise for the way the first years insisted on doing everything themselves.

There were tantrums and tears, naturally, they were artistic children after all and they hadn't got were they were today by being shrinking violets. Sophia wasn't happy about sharing the billing with Keira. She wanted a solo part, after all her mother had been...

"Oh shut up, Sophia," they all wailed at once.

In the end they decided on the *pas de trois* from *Sleeping Beauty* as it gave them all a chance to shine. Some had choreographed their own dances and Polly was to sing a solo. She had the kind of voice that brought tears to the eyes and had quickly earned herself the nickname of Polly Parrot. Not that she minded, she was a sweet girl and never happier than when she was singing.

Now that they were all happy with their choice rehearsals could get under way. Millie was in her element with all the costumes to design, she had written to her mother with details of anything she couldn't find at school and Mrs Martin had driven up one weekend with a carful of stuff left over from productions she had been involved in.

Valerie Martin was very much like her daughter, small with wiry hair and the energy of a rubber ball, happily bouncing from place to place and always with a smile on her face. She seemed to be permanently pinned into various colours of cloth as she whirled around trying costumes on people. She even turned up to ballet class one morning with a piece of red silk caught in the back of her leotard, much to everyone's amusement.

'The Show' as it was now generally known, was set for two weeks before Christmas. Excitement had risen to fever pitch throughout the Stageschool, many of the students were taking part in pantomimes, shows or concerts over the Christmas period, along with the general melee that went with the run up to the festive season it's not surprising that teacher's nerves were at breaking point and the whole place was reverberating with noise, colour and movement.

The first full rehearsal was due to take place on the Wednesday afternoon before the show and they had been given permission to use the theatre for three hours which didn't give them long. T.J was determined that everything would run smoothly, he had run up an order of appearance.

This resulted in a series of complaints from everyone, they either wanted to be first, or last, in the first Act or definitely in the second until poor T.J threw the list down onto the stage and told them all they would either do it his way or not at all.

Silence followed as no one really wanted to take over from him so they all agreed, with various degrees of reluctance, to stick to the schedule set. With only a week to go there was no time to do anything else.

Parents had been invited, the theatre booked, posters made and there was only two days to go. The costumes were ready and the music organised by Leon, poor T.J was becoming a nervous wreck as the day drew steadily nearer.

Keira came across him sitting on the stage, his legs hanging over the front, his head in his hands.

163

"Are you okay," she asked, pulling herself up beside him.

"I'm exhausted," he replied. "It's been a lot of hard work."

"But you have done really well, everyone says so. The show will be brilliant. Have you enjoyed it?"

"Well, I guess so. But now I'm worried I will let everyone down. And all their parents coming an' all."

"It will be fine. Honest, T.J. Even the teachers are impressed, Monsieur Raymond told me so. They are all coming, even Madame. The tickets are all sold so we will have plenty of money for Leon. You have done really well."

"We have all worked hard," T.J replied. "Practising all hours of day and night and that's on top of everything else. Everyone's looking forward to it so much. I just wish my parents could be here but they are on tour at the moment."

"That's a shame, they would be really proud."

"That's the nature of this life," T.J added with a sigh. "The stage comes first; everything else has to be last. I have known that since I was a child. My parents were often away and had to leave me behind with my grandparents. Sometimes I travelled with them but it wasn't easy and they decided I needed some steady schooling."

"But why in England? Aren't there stage schools in America?"

"Sure. I went to one in the States a couple of years back. Then they decided to tour round Europe so they wanted to find somewhere over here. England was the easiest as I didn't have to learn another language. Also, they knew Madame Lewinsky from her dancing days, and her son before he was killed."

"I didn't know Madame had a son. And he was killed? How sad."

"Yes, he was a dancer too. They said he was another Nijinsky or Nureyev. Could *jété* like he was on wings. He was killed in some kind of an accident while he was travelling. It was in the news at the time, surprised you haven't heard of him. David Lewinsky."

"Of course! I remember reading about it in a book. Poor Madame, fancy losing a son like that. And one so talented. How old was he when he died?"

"Twenty? Thirty? He had trained in France that's why his name is pronounced the French way, *Daveed.* That's when Madame gave up dancing and became a teacher. She founded this school a few years later. It was as if she wanted to find another David, train another child to take the place of the one she had lost."

"In that case, we will make doubly sure the show is a success. We will do it for Madame and her son as well as Leon and his family."

"Thanks Keira, you've cheered me up now. I will do this for us all." And he leaned across and gave her a kiss on the cheek.

Keira could feel the blush spreading up her face from her neck and a warm feeling washed over her. She wouldn't just dance her best; she would dance her very, very best, for Madame, for her mother and for T.J.

Chapter twenty-one

Show day dawned fine and sunny. Cold and crisp but not a day to put anyone off travelling, for which many of the students were grateful. Some of the parents would be travelling a great distance to see their children put on a show and they all desperately wanted it to be a success.

Keira woke up with a tight feeling of nerves in her stomach, and then remembered why. Today was the day of the show and her mother was coming to see her dance properly for the first time. The *Silver Fairy* didn't count as her mother hadn't known it was her until after. This time she was actually coming to see her and it made her feel even more nervous than ever.

Would she still think dancing was just a complete waste of time and money? Would she even suggest that Keira would be better off back in a normal school? The very idea was terrifying. She loved the Stageschool and never wanted to leave. Well, not until she was old enough to be in a proper company of course.

Sophia was still asleep so Keira got up as quietly as she could, washed and dressed and made her way down to the cafeteria for breakfast.

Leon was already in there, sitting alone drinking a cup of black coffee. This time she didn't hesitate to approach him. He was one of the gang now. A bit gruff at times but that was his way. He was used to being an outsider and he found it hard to believe that at the Stageschool he was accepted on grounds of his dancing and not judged for any other reason. It had been something it had taken him a while to learn but here he was just Leon, the dancer, and he had proved he was an exceptional dancer.

"Hi," Keira had picked up a carton of orange juice on the way over.

"Hey Keira. How are you?"

"Nervous. What about you? Are your sisters coming tonight?"

"Yes, all four of them and my dad. They are really looking forward to it. I thought my dad might think it was charity but he thought it was cool when I told him that everyone wanted to help."

"That's great. It will be a great show too, everyone has worked so hard."

"Yes, especially T.J. Who would have thought he could have organised the whole thing just like that?"

"He's very talented."

Keira couldn't help blushing, remembering the kiss. It had only been a peck on the cheek but it was the first time she had been kissed by someone not in her immediate family. Grandmothers and aunties didn't count. Nor did Uncle Ned who had no teeth and wasn't a real uncle anyway, more a friend of the family.

"And all the teachers will be there, even Madame. I hope she likes it."

"Bound to."

Keira wondered about telling Leon what she had found out about Madame and her son but it seemed kind of private somehow. Perhaps it wasn't her place to mention it. For some reason she felt very protective of Madame.

"I don't think I can eat anything today."

"Me neither, but we will have to have something to keep up our energy levels. Shall I see if there's any porridge ready?"

The cafeteria was starting to fill up now. Being a Saturday a few of the students took advantage of the chance for a lie-in. Some of them had signed up for extra classes and, of course, several were involved in the various productions taking place locally.

The rest of the first years had started to arrive. T.J appeared next, followed by Matty and Nic. They all gathered around the table, nervously sipping black coffee and nibbling toast.

Keira came back with two bowls of porridge, one for her and one for Leon.

"How can you eat anything?" T.J asked. He was a great black coffee drinker.

"Porridge is good for you, a slow release of energy. It will last much longer than toast. I shall have a banana later and a tuna sandwich for lunch."

"I shall drink black coffee all day with spoons full of sugar for energy," T.J announced.

"Yuk! Anyway, sugar is fattening."

"Not with the amount of exercise I do every day. Right, I want to see everyone promptly at nine in the theatre for warm ups. Then we will do a run through, nothing too heavy. I want you to save all the energy for tonight."

"No problem!" Leon stated, jumping up. He would rather be dancing than sitting around thinking about tonight. And his number was very sassy, just what he was good at.

"Let's get started, the sooner the better. Ah, here's Ruby and Millie. Come on sleepy heads, we're meeting at the theatre in twenty minutes."

"It's alright for you," Millie declared. "I haven't slept a wink all night. My stomach really hurts."

They all turned and looked at her anxiously. The last thing they needed was someone falling ill just before the show.

"Have you seen the nurse?" Keira asked.

"No, but I might have to if it carries on."

"I'll take you," Ruby said. "She might let you lie down and give you a hot water bottle to put on your stomach. She did for me."

"Okay," Millie said. She did look pale and there were dark lines under her eyes.

"Your mum will be here at lunch time, won't she?" Ruby asked.

"Yes, she's bringing a couple more things for the costumes."

"Well, she can keep an eye on you then. Come on; let's go to the medical room."

"I hope she's alright," Keira said. They really needed Millie this evening. Although they had the foresight to rehearse a couple of extra numbers just in case of any mishap, no one could deal with the costumes like Millie could.

"Right, let's go," T.J announced, banging his fist on the table. "It's already nine and we need to get over to the theatre, we only have it for three hours this morning. Straight after lunch, full dress rehearsal at two, then a rest before the performance at seven."

Everyone hoped that the old adage about the worse the dress rehearsal was the better the performance would be because the rehearsal was an absolute disaster. Ana's dress tore during the flamenco and Millie had been

169

made to stay in the sick room by the matron so she was unable to mend it. Ruby had to practise the tap dance without Millie, which didn't have the same impact and Polly nearly lost her voice during the singing of *Ave Maria* so ended up having to mime in order to save her voice for the evening.

Poor T.J was nearly pulling his hair out by the time they finally finished the rehearsal at three. They were all ready for a well-earned rest but too nervous to relax and Leon was physically sick he was so wound up.

"Perhaps you had better go to the nurse too," Matty said, as he stood by watching Leon throw up in the boys' toilets.

"No, don't do that. She will make me lie down and then I won't be able to do the show tonight. My whole family are coming, that's why I'm so nervous, and of course, I keep thinking of mum. She would love to have been here."

"Of course," Matty agreed sympathetically. "She would be very proud of you."

He couldn't imagine not having his parents at the show tonight. They had supported him right from the start, when he had first said that he had wanted to sing and dance. He didn't know what he would have done if they had tried to stop him although he knew his father hadn't been all that keen at first. Being the only boy in the family they had expected him to do something a bit more rugged.

Mr Weston was an engineer and had spent many years of his life in the Navy. Mrs Weston worked as a school secretary and had more of an artistic leaning so it was reckoned that Matty must have got his talent from her. Neither of his sisters had shown an interest in the stage. Sarah, the eldest, was an extremely bright girl who already had her sights on University and Helen was horse-mad. Her life revolved around gymkhanas and pony clubs and involved Mrs Weston in a lot of ferrying around at the weekend. That left Mr Weston to see to Matty and he wasn't all that keen on hanging around outside ballet classes. Rugby was more his thing and he found the whole idea of dancing, unless it was something by the Rolling Stones of course, slightly effeminate.

"But dad," Matty had protested. "Do you realise how hard we have to work? It's practice, practice, practice, and even then you might not be good enough to get into the corps de ballet, let alone become a soloist. And there's so many things can go wrong, injury, getting too tall, too heavy. Ballet is not for cissies!"

Mr Weston remained unconvinced. Matty hoped that when he came to watch the show he might be persuaded otherwise. That's if the show was able to go on, what with sickness and disasters with props and costumes.

"How are you feeling now?" Matty asked Leon, who looked decidedly green about the gills.

"I think I will go and lie down," Leon said.

Matty helped him to his feet and he slushed his hands and face under the cold tap.

"I'll come up with you. Are you sure you don't want the nurse?"

"No, I'm fine. She might stop me dancing in the show."

Matty knew how much Leon was looking forward to it so he didn't try and persuade him again. He left him in his room and hurried back to the *chill out* area where everyone except Millie and Leon were waiting.

"How is he?" T.J asked.

"A bit queasy, he might be ok after a rest."

171

"Millie's feeling a bit better," Ruby said. "Matron has given her paracetemol. Her mum will be here soon and she's going to help with the costumes too."

"The show will go on!" T.J said. "Come on guys, this isn't going to beat us."

"I'm going for a walk," Keira said. "Some fresh air and a stroll round the gardens will be good."

"That sounds a plan," Matty agreed. "I will come too."

"And me!"

The whole class decided it would be a good idea to get out for a while to clear their heads and de-stress before the show.

The Stageschool was set in beautiful parklands, green lawns to the front and back, neat herbaceous borders and woodland area on the perimeter. The students were allowed to use these areas whenever they liked and summer days often found them stretched out on the grass in the sunshine. Being a Saturday there were plenty of people taking advantage of the unexpectedly bright weather, walking in small groups across the grass and through the trees.

Keira always thought there was something magical about a winter landscape and wished she could draw the skeletal branches as they scratched the pale blue sky. It would make a wonderful backdrop for a ballet.

"It's hard to believe it's nearly Christmas," Matty said. "We've been here a whole term already."

"Amazing, isn't it? It feels like we've been here forever."

"Yes," Keira agreed. "And I never thought I would get here in the first place."

She began to tell them about her audition and changing places with Lucy.

"Wow, you were lucky they let you stay," Sophia said. "Of course, I applied for the Stageschool years ago.

My dance teacher always said I showed exceptional potential and I had private lessons from the age of eight."

"Oh shut up Sophia, not everyone's as lucky as you. Some people have to work jolly hard to get their place. What about poor old Leon?"

Soon they were all reminiscing about their dancing experiences and the time passed quickly, they had almost forgotten about the show when T.J suddenly said,

"Hey guys, it's nearly five. We need to get something to eat. We can't eat too close to the show so we better get into the canteen now."

It was growing cold and had started to get dark but no one had noticed. They were the only people left in the gardens and they hurried back to the school in order to get into the warmth and light.

"I hope I don't catch a cold," Sophia said, worriedly.

"You won't. Look, there's Millie. She must be feeling better. And that must be her mum. Come on, let's join them."

Millie's mum was great at making everyone feel relaxed. They were soon chatting to her as if they had known her all their lives. She was the sort of person they all wanted as a mother; she treated them like adults not children.

Just as they were finishing their tea Leon came to join them.

"Are you ok?" T.J asked.

"Well, I'm feeling a lot better. I will just have some biscuits or something to nibble. I couldn't face anything else just now."

"Well, we're all here," T.J said with a grin. "Now let's get ready for the show and impress them all with our talent!"

173

Chapter twenty-two

There was a nervous hush backstage as everyone got into their places for the first act. They had decided to open with the *pas de trois* from Sleeping Beauty followed by Ana dancing a flamenco then Matty's comic dance with T.J and Leon closing the first act with a modern dance which consisted of them dressed in neon blue and dancing against a yellow background. Everyone agreed the effect was quite stunning.

Keira stood in her place in the wings. The sounds from the auditorium were muffled but she knew that the theatre was packed, the tickets had been sold out and there was a lot of interest throughout the school to see what the first years were up to. Most of the staff had said they would be there too, there was even a rumour that Madame might be there.

T.J hovered nervously backstage with a clipboard in his hand. He was also in charge of the music although they had roped in a senior, Blake Roberts, to operate the sound system as he had experience of working as a sound engineer at the local theatre. Blake had been quite happy to help when he realised how professional the first year's show was.

The music faded in. Keira, Nic and Sophia poised in the wings ready to sweep onto the stage as the curtain opened and take their places for the *pas de trois*. Keira felt a fizz of excitement, similar to a small electric shock passing through her body and then the music lifted her up and she took the first step, her tutu frothing around her and the world beyond the stage was forgotten.

Her steps were light and the music wrapped itself around her, lifting, stretching, floating. Nic was there, guiding, moving, prompting and Sophia twirled in step, the three of them forming a whole, complete until the last note faded and they sank into a deep curtsey on either side of Nic.

Applause filled the theatre and Keira realised it was the first time she had been applauded for herself, when she had danced the *Silver Fairy* everyone had thought it was Lucy dancing. Now the audience clapped and somewhere out there was her mother, watching her, clapping, hopefully proud of her daughter. Keira felt tears prickling the back of her eyes and she had to bite her lip to stop herself from bursting into tears.

It was probably the best moment of her life so far. As she swept another curtsey she decided that this was what it was all about. The reward for all the hours of work, the unrelenting practice, the aching muscles and painful toes and she knew it was what she wanted for the rest of her life.

The curtain closed and she found herself hugging Nic and Sophia, jumping up and down with a rush of adrenalin that made it hard to stop. T.J was waving his clipboard at them, telling them to get off the stage so Ana could get into place for her flamenco. The lights dimmed and the audience hushed as Keira, Nic and Sophia hurried off backstage ready to get changed for their next number and Ana took her place in her red and black flamenco dress. She poised head back, one arm up the other on her hip; even her fingers were tense, waiting for the music to release them. Keira couldn't help admiring her. She stood for a few minutes as Ana took her first steps, the music beating out a raw rhythm as she tapped her foot and twisted her wrists in a twirling movement that held the audience spellbound. Every movement, every facial expression held special meaning and the music moved her in a way Keira had never experienced before.

There was a pause as the last note faded away then a burst of applause ruptured the silence. Keira found herself joining in, she had never seen anything so stirring and she wanted to watch it all over again. She found she was shivering as she entered the tiny dressing room where Sophia was already changing out of her costume ready for the finale, *The Toy Shop,* where they were all various toys brought to life by the magical shop keeper, danced by Matty.

Keira hung up her tutu and wrapped herself in a large crossover cardigan, not wanting to change into her rag doll costume too early. Ana returned to the dressing room and Millie helped her out of her dress. It had a tight-fitting stretch bodice and several layers of flouncy skirt which seemed to move with a life of its own.

"You were amazing!" Keira said.

"Gracias. Me gusta bailer. Me gusta la musica. I love to dance."

"I wish I could dance like you."

"Me too," Ruby put in. She was beginning to feel decidedly mediocre after watching Keira and Sophia dance and now the colour and excitement of Ana's flamenco. She dabbed her face with a towel and noticed with the dismay the make-up that had smudged on it. She would have to do it again.

Millie was fussing over the costumes, fluffing out the tutus, shaking the sequins to make them sparkle, smoothing the fluffy cat costume that Chloe was wearing in the finale.

Ruby was re-applying her mascara, Sophia doing her hair, releasing it from a classical bun so she could plait it on either side of her face for her role as a Tiger Lily Princess in the finale.

Keira took in all the scene around her, the smell of the rosin powder mixed with hairspray and a faint aroma of sweat. The silent concentration on all their faces, the nervous buzz of tension that filled the room and the excitement being held in check as they waited for their turn to shine. She loved everything about it. This was what she wanted, this was her life. She couldn't imagine anything else.

The second act opened with Nic and Chloe's scene from Hamlet and was greeted by enthusiastic applause. The audience were well and truly on their side now. Polly's *Ave Maria* had every mother in the audience with tears in their eyes and Leon's street dance brought the house down with cheers and stomps and whistles.

All too soon they were taking their places in the toy shop for the finale.

The first tinkling notes of the piano brought a hush to the audience and Keira took her first wobbling steps as a rag doll. It was perfect. Everyone danced their solo and were greeted by a burst of spontaneous applause at the end. When they took the final line up the audience rose to their feet and cheered.

It was several moments before the applause died down and the curtain fell for the last time. Hugging each other and jumping up and down with excitement they suddenly realised that they could hear a voice speaking over the microphone. A familiar voice, low and authorative.

It was Madame.

"It's Madame," Sophia shrieked, then clapped her hand over her mouth as they all strained to hear what she was saying.

"...with much pride that I would like to thank the first years for this wonderful show. They have created it all by themselves, dances, costumes, music. Not only that, the hard work has all been done for a purpose, to help out a fellow student. This makes it doubly a feat worth our praise. It has been decided that the Stageschool will set up a fund to help one deserving pupil each term. This term it will go to Leon Knight. The fund will be called the *David Lewinsky Award*, in honour of my son, and I will be proud to offer it every year from now on."

The audience cheered this news and the first years realised they were being beckoned on the stage to stand beside Madame. It was an unforgettable moment for each of them as they found themselves on the stage with Madame in front of a cheering audience.

Keira found herself scanning the rows of people in front of her, trying to find her mother amongst the sea of faces, but it was hard to pick out anyone amongst the shadowy figures. She had to be there, she had said she was coming.

It seemed that everyone wanted to hold on to the moment. No one wanted to change out of their costumes, parents rushed backstage, other students wanted to congratulate and join in the general melee. Leon was engulfed in a wave of family members and even the staff were mingling with the students in a cloud of euphoria.

Keira was swept along with the rest of the class and found herself amongst the audience. Then she spotted her mother who, to her surprise, was talking to Madame at the back of the theatre.

Oh no! She hoped she wasn't in any trouble. As she wound her way through the throng she realised her mother was crying. What could be the matter? A tight hand squeezed around her throat and she felt a rising tide of panic.

It seemed an age before she finally fought her way through the throng and was by her mother's side.

"Mum! Mum! What's wrong?"

Mrs Lewis dabbed her eyes with a handkerchief and put her arm around Keira's shoulder.

"Nothing, darling," she managed to say.

It was Madame who placed a calming hand on Keira's shoulder.

"You're mother has had some surprising news. Would you like me to explain?" She addressed the question to Mrs Lewis, who nodded slowly.

"You see, Keira. My son, David, was an aspiring dancer. He trained in Paris and was set to become as great as Nureyev. Sadly, he was killed in an accident leaving behind a wife and baby daughter. I had never met the daughter because the mother disappeared after the accident and I never heard from her again. Until today. Keira, you are that baby, David's daughter. You are my granddaughter."

Keira couldn't take it in. What was Madame trying to tell her? It couldn't be true. She looked to her mother, waiting for a further explanation.

"It's true," she whispered. "I was married to David Lewinsky, but he was known as Lewis then. David Lewinsky is your father."

For a moment Keira felt dizzy, everything was swirling around in her head. Nothing made sense. Then it all made perfect sense. Why her mother hadn't wanted her to dance. It was because of what had happened to her father.

179

Killed in an accident. What sort of accident? Did it have something to do with ballet? No wonder her mother didn't want her to dance.

Keira looked from one to the other of them and she knew it was true. Madame Lewinsky was her grandmother. Her father was a ballet dancer. No wonder she had felt this urge in her to always want to dance, from being a small child it was the only thing that had ever meant anything to her. Now she understood, it was in her blood.

Slowly the room came back into focus. Several faces were watching them curiously. What would the rest of the Stageschool make of it all? She thought of Sophia and her constant boasting about her mother, who no one had ever heard of. Keira didn't want anyone to think she was big headed like that.

"Please Madame; don't say anything about this to anyone."

"Of course not, I understand. You need time to come to terms with it yourself. I will say nothing. In the meantime, your mother and I will go to my office for some private talk. You return to your friends. You should all be very proud of yourselves tonight. Well done to all of you."

"Thank you, Madame."

Keira bobbed a little curtsey as she had been trained to do and hurried over to where she could see Ruby and Millie with Millie's mum. She needed to lose herself in the excitement of the moment and forget about the news she had just received until she could work it out for herself.

"What was Madame talking to you about?" Millie asked curiously.

"Oh, just about the show. She said well done to all of us. Wasn't it just amazing?"

It didn't take much for the topic of conversation to turn back to the show and to carry on well into the night. Normal rules were relaxed, parents stayed with their children and no one was in their rooms by lights out. The buzz just went on and on.

Leon and his family had become the centre of attention but Keira and her mother had found a quiet corner to sit in Madame's office where they had been left to talk things over.

They were both in tears and Keira had the photograph of David Lewinsky in front of her taken from Madame's shelf.

"Why didn't you tell me?" she asked her mother.

"It was such a long time ago. I didn't want you to know about your father."

"But I wanted to know. He was my father after all. Is that why you tried to stop me dancing?"

"It's all such a long time ago now, Keira. Your father and I were very young when we first met. He was dancing in the corps de ballet of the Paris Opera at the time and they were on tour in London. I had been working there as a nanny and met him in a cafe one lunch time. It was what they called a whirlwind romance, by the time I realised I was pregnant he had moved back to Paris. I contacted him. We got married but I always felt he would resent me if I held him back from dancing. Dancing always came first with David. That's why I resented it so much. And when he was killed in that stupid accident I always felt like it was dancing that had killed him. He was travelling back from a show very late at night and the car hit ice on the road.

After the funeral I just wanted to get as far away from everything as possible. I moved back to be near my mum. I didn't want to have anything to do with ballet, or with Madame or that side of the family at all. I never told her where we were or anything about you.

When you started on about wanting to dance it was quite a shock to me. Just like your dad all over again."

"I'm sorry mum."

"It's not your fault, darling." Lauren sighed heavily. "I guess it's in your blood. But now you know."

"So, I take after my father."

It was a scary thought. A man she had never even met was somehow influencing her life. She stared at the photograph. It was faded now. It was hard to make out the features on his face but he seemed to have a dreamy look about him, not unlike Keira herself when she was in one of her far away moods. His eyes were dark and seemed to be looking at Keira from the depths of the picture. As if he knew she was looking at him. The daughter he had never met.

"I'm sorry, darling. I know it's all been a shock to you today. But when I heard Madame announce about the David Lewinsky prize it all came flooding back and I couldn't stop crying. One of the teachers asked if I was alright, then Madame came over. She realised who I was straight away. I think she must have known who you were but she never said anything to you. I guess she wanted to see how you would get on on your own, without the help of having famous relatives in the ballet world."

Keira thought of Sophia and her constant boasting and knew she didn't want to be like her. She would ask Madame not to tell anyone about this. She wanted to be a dancer because she was good at it, not because of who her father or grandmother were.

Nevertheless, it made her all the more determined. She would be a dancer. She would be the best that she could.   Not just for herself, but for her mother and father, and for Madame too.

Keira had never been so glad that she had come to the Stageschool as she was just now.   She was going to work hard, every minute of every day, and she would be a ballet dancer.

She was convinced, that was what she was born for and she knew she would succeed.   The future stretched out in front of her like a golden path.

Cast

Keira Lewis
Ruby Soames
Millie Martin
Sophia Petit
Ana Garcia
Chloe Taylor
Chloe Brown
Polly Wilson

T.J Smith
Leon Knight
Matty Weston
Nic Herrington

Find Keira and her friends in:

Keira at Stageschool
Mystery at Stageschool
Stageschool by the Sea
Summer at Stageschool
Stageschool on Tour
Stageschool in Spain
Last term at Stageschool

CPSIA information can be obtained at www.ICGtesting.com
Printed in the USA
BVOW07s1127050813

327861BV00001B/5/P